She glanced at him, feeling tears spring to her eyes when she saw the expression on his face.

That he was deeply moved by his first sight of their child wasn't in doubt, and something inside her seemed to open up at the thought. For five long years she had tried her best to blank out the memory of that night. Now she realised that it would be impossible not to think about it.

She and Vincenzo had made love that night, and by doing so they had created this precious child—a child who desperately needed their help if she was to survive. While she had always been prepared to do whatever was necessary to save Megan, she had never expected that Vincenzo would feel the same.

She bit her lip as a wave of panic swamped her. Maybe the situation hadn't changed. Maybe it was still the same in many ways. However, knowing that Vincenzo cared what happened to Megan made a world of difference to how she felt about him. Making love again with Vincenzo wouldn't be merely a means to an end now. It would be so much more…

Dear Reader

Last year I was fortunate enough to enjoy a holiday in the Italian Lakes. I stayed in a beautiful old villa, which had been converted into a hotel, overlooking Lake Garda. It was the perfect spot for a holiday and I thoroughly enjoyed exploring the area.

One day when I was taking the ferry across the lake I spotted a young couple with their child. They were such an attractive family, although it was obvious that the little boy had been ill. They were on the ferry again when I set off back to Garda later that afternoon and I got talking to the child's mother, who turned out to be English. She told me that they were having a holiday with her in-laws. Her son *had* been extremely ill, and they were hoping that fresh air and sunshine would help him regain his strength. We parted company soon afterwards, but what she told me stayed with me and triggered the idea for this book: what lengths would a woman go to if it meant she could save her child?

I really enjoyed writing Lowri's and Vincenzo's story. They are two strong characters who met by chance and now find themselves united in their desire to save their child. What neither expects is that they will find themselves falling in love during the process!

I hope you enjoy this book as much as I enjoyed writing it.

Best wishes to you all

Jennifer

SAVING HIS
LITTLE MIRACLE

BY
JENNIFER TAYLOR

Published in Great Britain 2014
by Mills & Boon, an imprint of Harlequin (UK) Limited,
Eton House, 18-24 Paradise Road, Richmond, Surrey, TW9 1SR

© 2014 Jennifer Taylor

ISBN: 978 0 263 24377 2

Harlequin (UK) Limited's policy is to use papers that are natural, renewable and recyclable products and made from wood grown in sustainable forests. The logging and manufacturing processes conform to the legal environmental regulations of the country of origin.

Printed and bound in Great Britain
by CPI Antony Rowe, Chippenham, Wiltshire

Jennifer Taylor lives in the north-west of England, in a small village surrounded by some really beautiful countryside. She has written for several different Mills & Boon® series in the past, but it wasn't until she read her first Medical Romance™ that she truly found her niche. She was so captivated by these heart-warming stories that she set out to write them herself! When she's not writing, or doing research for her latest book, Jennifer's hobbies include reading, gardening, travel, and chatting to friends both on and off-line. She is always delighted to hear from readers, so do visit her website at www.jennifer-taylor.com

Recent titles by Jennifer Taylor:

MR RIGHT ALL ALONG
THE MOTHERHOOD MIX-UP
THE REBEL WHO LOVED HER*
THE SON THAT CHANGED HIS LIFE*
THE FAMILY WHO MADE HIM WHOLE*
GINA'S LITTLE SECRET
SMALL TOWN MARRIAGE MIRACLE
THE MIDWIFE'S CHRISTMAS MIRACLE
THE DOCTOR'S BABY BOMBSHELL**
THE GP'S MEANT-TO-BE BRIDE**
MARRYING THE RUNAWAY BRIDE**
THE SURGEON'S FATHERHOOD SURPRISE†

*Bride's Bay Surgery
**Dalverston Weddings
†Brides of Penhally Bay

Dedication

For Vicky, a wonderful mother and
a wonderful daughter too.

CHAPTER ONE

HAD SHE MADE a mistake by coming here?

Lowri Davies took a deep breath as she watched the taxi drive away. It was too late to be having second thoughts at this stage. If there had been another option open to her, she would have taken it months ago. However, the fact was that Vincenzo was the only person who could help her.

If he would.

A shiver ran through her at the thought of what she was going to ask him to do. It might have been easier if she'd had some idea of how he would react but she knew too little about him to predict his response. All they'd had were those few weeks together and it hadn't been enough to get to know what sort of a person he really was. Would he agree or would he refuse to get involved? The fact that he hadn't replied to her letter didn't bode well but she couldn't let that deter her. She needed his help, needed it *desperately* if she hoped to save Megan!

Lifting her hand, Lowri pressed the button on the intercom speaker. The villa was huge, much bigger than she had expected it would be. Built on the hillside overlooking the glittering waters of Lake

Garda, it was an imposing property. Through the ornate wrought-iron gates she could see immaculately tended grounds and grimaced. Although it had been apparent even from the brief time they had spent together that Vincenzo was wealthy, she hadn't realised just how rich he was.

A house like this must cost a small fortune to maintain, and then there was his apartment in an exclusive part of Milan as well. Even a top surgeon like Vincenzo couldn't afford two such properties on his salary. He had to have private means, family money that helped to pay for this kind of luxurious lifestyle. The thought was unsettling. The last thing she wanted was him thinking that she was after his money.

'*Sì?*'

The sound of a deeply masculine voice coming through the speaker made her jump. Lowri pressed her hand to her racing heart. It was five years since she had seen Vincenzo and she'd not had any contact with him since yet she had no difficulty recognising his voice. It was as though it had imprinted itself into her brain and lain there, dormant, for all that time. Now all of a sudden it had awoken a lot of memories, especially of that last night they had spent together...

'Vincenzo, it's Lowri,' she said quickly, not wanting to go down that route. Nothing would change what had happened that night, the same as it wouldn't change what had happened afterwards. She and Vincenzo had slept together and there had been unforeseen consequences.

'Lowri?'

He repeated her name, his voice holding the faintest hint of puzzlement, and Lowri felt her cheeks burn with embarrassment. Had he forgotten her, erased her so completely from his memory that he didn't even recognise her name? If truth be told, she was probably just one of many women he had slept with. No more and no less than that.

'Lowri Davies,' she said, feeling her temper inch its way up the scale. Maybe she was merely another notch on his bedpost but he could hardly claim not to remember her after that letter she had sent him. It made her wonder if it was all an act aimed at getting rid of her. Well, if that was the case, he was in for a shock.

'You must remember me, Vincenzo. Whilst I'm sure there've been a lot of women in your life, I doubt if many have written to tell you they were expecting your child.' She gave a brittle little laugh. 'Does that ring any bells?'

Vincenzo Lombardi felt the air rush from his lungs. Just for a moment, he stood stock still and stared at the entryphone. Was this some sort of a sick joke?

Oh, he remembered her all right, remembered her far better than he would have expected. All they'd had were those few weeks yet he could recall with perfect clarity every second of the time they had spent together. He closed his eyes, surprised by the speed with which he conjured up her image: light brown hair falling softly to her shoulders; hazel eyes that could turn from green to gold according to her mood. Her body had been slender but womanly with full breasts and a narrow waist.

His own body gave its pronouncement on that memory and his eyes shot open. What in heaven's name was he doing? He should be focusing on what she had said, not on how he had felt when they had made love.

'I have no idea what you're talking about, *signorina*. If this is some sort of a joke then it is in very poor taste.'

'It isn't a joke. I wrote to you a couple of months after we'd spent that night together, as soon as I discovered I was pregnant, in fact. Are you claiming that you never received my letter?'

The scorn in her voice made his face burn. Vincenzo stared at the receiver again, stunned that she could have this effect on him. It had been years since he had blushed, years since he had felt anything akin to shame. He had trained himself not to show his emotions, not to feel them most of the time even. He knew that his colleagues at the hospital in Milan considered him to be cold and arrogant but it didn't worry him. In his view, it was better to be in control than to suffer all the emotional traumas they did.

'I am not claiming anything, *signorina*. I never received any letter from you. That is a fact. Now, I'm sorry but I don't have the time to continue this discussion.'

Vincenzo replaced the receiver in its rest. Picking up the towel that he had tossed over the back of a chair, he headed to the bathroom. He had overdone things today and his body was aching from the punishing routine he had put it through, but the only way he was going to regain full fitness was by pushing himself. It had been six months since the skiing accident that had caused such havoc in his life and he needed to step up his training if he hoped to get back into Theatre. Surgery was his raison d'être, the thing that gave him the most pleasure. He couldn't imagine how empty his life would be if he couldn't do it any more.

The sound of the intercom buzzing brought him up short. Vincenzo swung round and glared at the receiver. So she hadn't gone away. She was still here, still intent on perpetuating that ridiculous lie. Tossing the towel onto the floor, he strode out of the room, determined that he was going to put an end to this situation. He had no idea why she had decided to come here and make that ridiculous claim but he wasn't going to be a party to it. If Lowri Davies had had a child, it certainly wasn't his!

She was standing outside the gates when Vincenzo left the house and he slowed when he saw her. All of a sudden he felt the need to prepare himself and it was a surprise to feel that way. His confidence was legendary, his self-assurance absolute. He *always* knew what to do even when presented with the most difficult of situations, yet for some reason he felt unsure about how to handle this.

After all, there had to be a reason why she had come here today. It had been five years since he had seen her and if she'd had a child in that time, he or she must be at least four years old. So why had she left it until now to make that claim about him being the father? Intuition warned him that there was more to her visit than first appeared, although he had no idea what it might be. He would have to rely on his instincts to deal with this and if there was one thing Vincenzo hated it was trusting to luck. He preferred his life to be free of surprises, mapped out to the nth degree. That way there was less chance of him getting hurt.

The thought stunned him, mainly because it was the first time he had admitted that he might be vulnerable in any way. Vincenzo's mouth thinned as he strode down the path. Maybe his self-control wasn't as absolute as he had believed, but it was good enough to deal with this unwelcome intrusion. It made no difference why Lowri Davies had come to see him. Whatever her motives were, he had no intention of being manipulated!

Lowri could feel her heart pounding as she watched Vincenzo stride down the path. That he was less than pleased to see her was obvious but she wouldn't let that deter her. In a fast sweep her eyes ran over him, taking stock of the changes the past five years had wrought.

Physically he had changed very little, she decided. His black hair was as thick and lustrous as ever, his skin gleaming with good health and vitality. He was wearing black running shorts cut high at the sides with a black vest and she could see that his body was still taut and honed.

It was only as he drew closer that she realised how much older he looked, older and even more self-contained. There had always been an aloofness about him, a tendency to distance himself from other people, and it was more apparent than ever these days. He looked cold and remote and far from happy about her turning up like this but it was hard luck. She didn't care how he felt. She only cared about what he could do for Megan.

'I don't know why you've come here and I don't wish to know either. However, let me make myself clear: if you've had a child, Signorina Davies, it has nothing to do with me.'

Lowri had to stop herself taking a step back as he stared at her through the gate. The coldness in his eyes was far more intimidating than anger would have been. Vincenzo had always been in control. Even though she had known him only for a short time, she had soon realised that he kept his emotions on a very tight rein—apart from that night when they had made love.

The thought sent a rush of heat through her and Lowri shuddered. She had tried not to think about that night. It had seemed pointless dwelling on it, foolish to imagine that it had meant anything to Vincenzo when his subsequent actions had proved that it hadn't.

They had slept together for comfort, out of mutual need even, but that was all. It hadn't been the start of something, neither had she wanted it to be. She had been in a bad place at the time, still struggling to come to terms with her ex-fiancé's deception, and that was why she had slept with Vincenzo...

Wasn't it?

The thought brought her up short. Lowri realised that she was in danger of allowing herself to be side-tracked and that would never do. She had come here for one reason and one reason alone—to help Megan. Their daughter. She squared her shoulders in readiness for the battle that lay ahead. Even though Vincenzo might refuse to accept that Megan was his child, there was no doubt in Lowri's mind about her daughter's parentage.

'She. We have a daughter, Vincenzo. Her name is Megan and she was four years old in March.'

Opening her bag, Lowri took out the first of the photographs she had brought with her, her heart aching as she looked at her daughter's smiling face and recalled how different Megan had looked yesterday when she had left her with her sister, Cerys. She didn't care what Vincenzo thought about her, didn't care if his life was about to be disrupted either. She only cared about this child they had created. Saving Megan was the most important thing of all.

Her eyes met his as she held up the picture so that he couldn't avoid seeing it. Oh, he might wish to dispute his parentage but anyone looking at the photograph could see in an instant how like him Megan was. The little girl had the same thick black hair and light olive skin, the same deep grey eyes. Even her nose was a smaller version of Vincenzo's, arrow straight without even the hint of a tilt at the end of it. Apart from her mouth—which was like Lowri's— Megan was the image of him and Lowri dared him to dispute it.

'You can see from this that Megan is your child, Vincenzo. But if it isn't enough to convince you then we can arrange to have DNA tests done. I have brought samples with me so you can send them off to a lab of your choice.'

She paused, waiting for him to say something, but he just stood there, staring impassively at the photograph. He seemed unmoved by the evidence she was showing him, uncaring even if Megan was his child or not, and her temper leapt a little further up the scale. 'It will be harder to argue with the results of them, I imagine.'

'What do you want?'

His voice was low yet Lowri flinched as though he had shouted the question at her. She took a quick breath, feeling her heart fluttering wildly inside her chest. The thought of what she was about to ask him to do made her feel sick, but she mustn't think about how she felt, but about what it could mean for Megan.

'It's quite simple, Vincenzo. I want us to have another child.'

CHAPTER TWO

'IF YOU WOULD wait in here, my housekeeper will bring you something to drink while I get changed. Which would you prefer: tea or coffee?'

'Neither. I didn't come here to sit around drinking tea, Vincenzo. I have more important things to worry about!'

Vincenzo heard the mounting hysteria in Lowri's voice and inwardly flinched. He hated scenes, hated any display of unbridled emotion. Swinging round on his heel, he strode to the door, determined that he wasn't going to be drawn into a discussion until she calmed down. They needed to talk about this calmly and rationally.

If that was possible.

His stomach roiled as he recalled what she had said. She had asked him to have another child with her and if that weren't proof of her state of mind, what was? Even setting aside that claim she had made about him being the father of her daughter, what sane woman would have asked that of him? No, she was completely overwrought, unbalanced even, and he needed to proceed with the utmost caution if he was to avoid an ugly confrontation.

'Don't walk away from me, Vincenzo! I'm sorry if I've disrupted your day by coming here, but you're going to listen to what I have to say whether you like it or not!'

Vincenzo came to an abrupt halt when she caught hold of his arm. Her fingers were icily cold against his bare skin and he fought to suppress the shiver that ran through him. Turning, he stared into her angry face, his lips already parted to remonstrate with her. Nobody ordered him about; he wouldn't allow them to. Even if she was undergoing some sort of a mental crisis, she needed to understand that. However, for some reason he found the harsh words drying up when he looked into her eyes and saw the fear they held.

'I need your help, Vincenzo, not for me but for Megan. That's why I'm here. Because there's nothing else I can do for her.'

She let go of his arm and he saw the shudder that passed through her. It struck him then just how terrified she looked. Maybe she wasn't behaving rationally but it was obvious that she was under a huge amount of strain. The thought made him reconsider his decision to get rid of her as quickly as possible. Maybe they had known each other only for a very short time but she had helped him through a difficult period in his life. He owed it to her to listen to what she had to say at the very least.

Vincenzo turned and made his way to the sofa, surprised that he felt this way. He rarely felt under an obligation and couldn't remember the last time he had put someone else's needs before his own. However, there was something about the fear in Lowri's hazel eyes that touched a chord inside him. He wanted to help her even though he had no idea why.

'Thank you.'

Her voice was soft, filled with a relief that made his skin prickle in atavistic response. It was as though it had sliced through all the layers that had built up over the years and cut right to the very heart of him. Vincenzo took a deep breath, feeling oddly disorientated. He always knew how to behave in any situation, was always able to harness his emotions and steer them in the direction he wanted them to go, but not now. Not when he could tell how much it meant to her to have him do her bidding.

'The fact that I am willing to listen to you means nothing,' he said harshly, hating the fact that he felt so vulnerable. It was such an alien feeling and one he didn't intend to foster either.

'Maybe not, but it's a start.'

She gave him a quick smile as she sat down and Vincenzo felt his own mouth start to curl in imitation of hers before he stopped it. Leaning back against the cushions, he stared coldly back at her, needing to set the tone for how the conversation would continue. Maybe she hoped to persuade him to agree to her request by employing all her charm, but there was no way that it was going to happen. He had never wanted children and he wasn't about to change his mind...although if what she had said *was* true, perhaps it was already too late to turn his back on fatherhood.

The thought sent a chill coursing through him. Vincenzo shifted uncomfortably in his seat. Although he was loath even to consider the idea that he might be the child's father, he had to admit that she looked a lot like him. What if she was his daughter? What was he going to do then?

He had sworn that he would never have a family. His own less than idyllic childhood had put him off the idea. His mother had died shortly before his second birthday and he didn't remember her at all. His father had brought him up and he had made it abundantly clear how much he had resented the time he'd had to spend with him.

Vincenzo had taken his lead from that. In his view, children needed far too much time and attention. He had seen how his colleagues struggled to balance the demands of family life with their work and he had vowed that he would never place himself in the same position. His job came first and everything else a very poor second. He didn't have the time or the inclination to raise a family and he needed to make that clear before they went any further. Even in the unlikely event that the child turned out to be his, he didn't intend to get involved.

'I need to make my position perfectly clear, Signorina Davies. If what you say is correct, and it does turn out that I am the child's father, I have no intention of getting involved in her life. Quite simply, children are not on my agenda and they never will be.'

He stared at Lowri, waiting for her to react, but her expression didn't alter and, strangely enough, he wished that it had. It would have been that much easier to know what to say next if she had reacted with anger or incredulity even. He cleared his throat, feeling his stomach churning because he suddenly found himself in the unwelcome position of having to second-guess what she was thinking.

'I am willing to have the DNA tests done if it means they will resolve this matter. If they prove that I am the father then naturally I shall make arrangements regarding the child's support. However, that is where my involvement ends. I have no desire to play any role whatsoever in her life, you must understand.'

'I do. I understand perfectly. However, I didn't come here to ask you for money, Vincenzo. I am more than capable of supporting our daughter without your help.'

Her voice held a disdain that made Vincenzo's skin heat with embarrassment. It was as though he had been put to the test and found wanting and it wasn't a pleasant feeling. He stared back at her, doing his best to rein in the odd mix of emotions that filled him. Anger and shame weren't things he was used to feeling and he didn't appreciate the fact that she could trigger such a response in him.

'You say that now but who's to say you won't change your mind at some point? If I am the child's father then I shall instruct my lawyers to draw up the appropriate papers.' He shrugged, feeling easier now that he was back in control of the conversation. 'If you don't wish to use the money, it can be put into a trust fund for the child to use in the future.'

'Megan. Her name is Megan. Referring to her as *the child* won't change anything, Vincenzo. She's still your daughter!'

Lowri glared at him. If she'd had a choice she would have got up right then and left, but she didn't have a choice, did she? She needed his help so she had to stay, had to persuade him to do what she wanted.

Her stomach rolled as it struck her how unlikely it

was that he would agree. Even though she had known from the outset that it had been a long shot, she had hoped that she might be able to convince him to help her. Now, after what he had said about children not being on his agenda, it seemed less likely than ever. The thought that she might have failed brought a rush of tears to her eyes but she blinked them away. She wouldn't give up, not yet, not until she had done everything possible to persuade him.

Reaching into her bag, she took out a second photograph. It had been taken the previous week, shortly after Megan had been allowed home from hospital. Despite the fact that she had been exhausted, Megan was smiling as she held up the new doll Lowri had bought for her. She'd been so brave, Lowri thought, running her fingertip over the glossy surface of the photograph. Megan had been through so much in her short life yet she had still found the courage to smile for the camera. Now *she* had to be just as brave if she was to have any hope of saving her beloved daughter.

She laid the photograph on the coffee table then placed the first one next to it, her heart aching as she compared the two. Nobody looking at these pictures could fail to be moved by what they saw and she could only pray that Vincenzo's heart would be touched too.

'This was taken last week when Megan came home from hospital,' she explained, her voice catching. She cleared her throat, knowing that she couldn't afford to break down. She needed to persuade him to help her and to do that she had to be coherent, had to lay out her arguments in a logical sequence and convince him that it was the right thing to do.

The thought of what she wanted from him made

her heart race but she ignored it. She would worry about that later; think about what it would entail after she had done this.

'She lost her hair after the chemotherapy but we're going to get her a wig as soon as I get back home.' She gave a little laugh, stopping the instant she felt it start to turn into a sob. 'Apparently, she wants a bright pink one, just like her favourite doll, so we should have fun choosing it.'

'What's wrong with her?' Vincenzo's voice was still cool, but Lowri heard the catch in it he tried so hard to hide and felt relief pour through her. So he wasn't totally impervious to their daughter's plight after all!

It took every scrap of strength she could muster to keep her own voice steady; however, she knew that he would retreat behind that wall he had erected between himself and the world if she showed too much emotion, and then wondered how on earth she could possibly know that. They'd spent just three weeks together, twenty-one days, and it hadn't been enough to get to know him properly, yet she knew in her heart that emotion scared him.

Her voice softened, took on the same soothing note she used with Megan whenever she was afraid. 'Acute lymphoblastic anaemia. She was diagnosed last year, on her third birthday, in fact, and she's had almost a full year of treatment.'

'Is she in remission?' he asked bluntly.

'Yes.' Lowri tried not to read anything into the fact that he sounded less shocked this time. 'However, I've been warned that it's unlikely to last and that the cancer will return. Her consultant explained that her best hope is a stem-cell transplant. It's highly effective in young children like Megan and it could mean that she's cured.'

'And have you found a donor?'

'No. There's nobody on the bone-marrow register who's a match. I've been tested, of course, and my sister as well. Her two boys, Ben and Dan, have also been tested.' She smiled as she thought about her nephews. 'Ben's fifteen and Daniel's only thirteen but they insisted on being tested if it meant they might be able to help Megan. They adore her, see her more as a little sister than a cousin, in fact, but neither of them are a suitable match, sadly. Our best hope of finding a donor is if she had a sibling.'

'Which is why you came to see me,' Vincenzo said flatly.

He looked up, his eyes meeting hers, and Lowri felt a trickle of heat run down her spine when she saw the way he was looking at her. All of a sudden she knew that he was remembering that night they had slept together and her breath caught as her own head was suddenly filled with memories: the desire in Vincenzo's eyes as he drew her down onto the bed; the coolness of his hands as he stroked her body; the heat of their sweat-slick skin as they clung to each other in the final seconds before the world dissolved in a shower of stars…

She stood up abruptly, desperate to break the visual contact. She had tried not to think about that night, had tried her hardest to erase it from her mind. There had seemed no reason to think about it after Vincenzo had ignored her letter so every time she had been tempted to recall what had happened, she had driven the thoughts away. Now all she could think about was how she had felt when they had made love. Vincenzo had aroused her passion to a level it had never reached before. She had wanted him more than she had wanted anyone, even Jonathan, her ex, and the thought stunned her.

She hadn't been in love with Vincenzo. She couldn't possibly have been in love with him! She had known him for too short a time and known him only on the surface too, not known *him*, the person he was underneath. It would be madness to imagine there was a bond between them. The only link that existed was their daughter and that was all there would ever be.

Unless he agreed to help her and they conceived another child. A child who might save Megan's life. A child who might also forge a stronger bond between them.

Vincenzo stepped into the shower, letting the hot water pound down onto his head. Would it clean his mind as well as his body? he wondered. Wash away the thoughts that were running riot inside his head?

That was why he had excused himself and left Lowri in the *salone*, drinking the tea his housekeeper had made for them. He couldn't have drunk a single drop; he had realised that and made his escape. He had run away, distanced himself from a situation he didn't know how to handle, and it didn't make him feel good to know that he had been a coward.

All his adult life he had prided himself on knowing what to do and doing it, on making a decision and sticking to it. But he had no idea what he was going to do about this. Lowri wanted him to give her another child, a child who might help to save the daughter he had known nothing about until today. Quite frankly, it was too much to take in!

Vincenzo swore under his breath as he stepped out of the stall. Drying himself on one of the huge white bath towels, he strode into his bedroom and flung open the wardrobe doors. He needed clothes that would say the right thing, give the right impression. Running shorts and a vest certainly hadn't helped. He needed something more formal, clothes that would help to protect his mind as well as cover his body. He needed to feel like *himself* when he saw Lowri again, not like this person he had turned into, the one who couldn't make decisions.

What if he refused and Megan died—how would he feel then? Could he live with the thought that he might have been able to save her?

His hand stilled. He could feel his heart thumping, feel the blood pounding in his temples. He had sworn a solemn oath when he had qualified as a doctor that he would do everything in his power to uphold life, yet he was contemplating letting his own child die.

What sort of a man did that make him? What kind of a person? Maybe he hadn't expected to find himself in this position but if it was true, if the child *was* his, how could he turn his back on her? Yet if he did agree, and he and Lowri had another child, what kind of an impact would it have on his life? Would he be able to cope with fatherhood or would he turn out exactly like his own father had been, full of resentment and bitterness? Did he really want any child to have to endure the sort of loveless childhood he'd had?

His face was set as he reached into the wardrobe

and took out a pair of chinos. He slipped them on then opened a drawer and pulled out a T-shirt and dragged it over his head. What he wore was irrelevant. What mattered more was that he did what was right, not just what was right for him but right for them all—him, Lowri and Megan. His daughter.

His breath caught because it was no longer a question of maybe but definitely. He knew the child was his flesh and blood, knew it with a certainty that would have shocked him before today. He never accepted anything at face value normally. He always checked that any facts presented to him were correct. However, in his heart he *knew* that Megan was his daughter and the fact that he was prepared to accept it as the truth scared him. If he relied on emotions rather than proof, he would never be in control of this situation.

Vincenzo left the bedroom, taking his time as he made his way downstairs while he assembled his thoughts. Instinct was all well and good but he refused to allow it to take over. There was a lot to discuss if he and Lowri were to work out a solution to this dilemma.

His mind skipped ahead, presenting him with a scene that made his blood heat, and he groaned. Thinking about making love to Lowri was the last thing he should be doing when he needed a clear head! He took a steadying breath then opened the door to the *salone*, frowning when he discovered the room was empty. Where was she? Surely she hadn't left?

He swung round then stopped when he saw her crossing the hall. She was wearing a sundress, pale green cotton with narrow straps at the shoulders and a full skirt. Vincenzo found himself thinking how much it suited her, the colour bringing out the golden lights in her brown hair and making her hazel eyes appear greener than ever. With it she was wearing a pair of leather sandals and he felt his stomach muscles clench when he saw the gleam of fresh polish on her toenails. For some reason he found it incredibly touching that she had dressed with such care for this meeting. Lowri was prepared to do anything it took to save her daughter. Even if it meant sleeping with him. Now he had to decide if he was as brave as her.

CHAPTER THREE

THEY SAT OUTSIDE on the terrace. Lowri much preferred it there to the stiff formality of the *salone* with its antique furniture and priceless *objets d'art* and she was glad when Vincenzo suggested it. Now, as she looked around the gardens, she felt some of the tension seep out of her. Maybe it was foolish to see it as a positive sign that he would agree to her request, but at least he was prepared to listen to her.

'Who's looking after the chil... Looking after *Megan* while you're here?'

Lowri's mouth curved into a tiny smile as he corrected himself. Another positive step. 'My sister, Cerys. She's looked after Megan since she was a baby when I went back to work.'

'You returned to work soon after she was born?' Vincenzo queried, his dark brows drawing into a frown.

'When she was six months old.' Lowri shrugged, refusing to let him see how guilty she felt about having to leave her daughter at such a tender age. 'Needs must, and I needed to work to support us.'

'I see.' He glanced across the lawn, his eyes resting on the glimmering vista of the lake just visible through the trees. 'So you and your fiancé didn't re-solve your differences?'

'No.' Lowri didn't elaborate. Although she had told Vincenzo the whole sorry tale five years ago, she didn't intend to go over it again. If she was honest, she still felt foolish about allowing Jonathan to deceive her. He had promised her the earth—a home and a family, the happily-ever-after every woman dreamt about. Unfortunately, the one thing he had failed to mention was that he was already married.

'It must have been difficult for you, Lowri. Working and caring for a baby can't have been easy. You must have resented being burdened with such a problem.' His voice was flat and she frowned, wondering at his choice of words.

'It hasn't been easy and especially not this past year. But Megan has never been a burden. She's the best thing that ever happened to me, if you want the truth.'

'Really?' He sounded so surprised that she frowned this time.

'Yes, really. She's a happy and contented little girl who gets up to all sorts of mischief.' She laughed. 'Last year I had the paddling pool out in the garden and she used her watering can to fill my wellies with water. I only realised it when I put them on!'

'And were you cross with her?' he asked, studying her face with an odd intensity.

'Of course not! I couldn't possibly have been cross when it was so funny.' Her expression sobered abruptly. 'I only wish she was well enough to get up to that sort of mischief these days.'

'She will be. I'm sure she'll be doing all sorts of naughty things very soon.'

He touched her hand, his fingers making only the briefest contact before he drew away, but Lowri still felt her breath catch. It was the first time he had willingly touched her since that night five years ago and she felt dizzy with the rush of sensations that thought aroused. She swallowed hard, forcing herself to focus on what was happening. There was no point dwelling on the past when it was the present that mattered. However, it appeared that Vincenzo still had questions he wanted answered.

'You said that you sent me a letter when you discovered you were pregnant. Was it true?'

'Of course it was true!' She sat up straighter, realising that she was in danger of forgetting just how tenuous her position really was. Whilst Vincenzo might seem more receptive to what she had to say, it wasn't a foregone conclusion that he would agree to help her.

She blanked out the thought of what would need to happen if he were to agree. It was stupid to feel even the slightest hint of distaste. She had thought it all through and she was sure that asking him to donate sperm was the best thing to do. After all, she knew nothing about his life these days, if he was in a relationship or had remarried even. The last thing she wanted was to create problems for him so artificial insemination seemed like the best way forward.

Anyway, she certainly didn't intend to sleep with him again. She had been bitterly hurt by his rejection and had no intention of placing herself in the same position again, even though, if she was honest, it hadn't been an unpleasant experience at the time. Her cheeks burned at the thought and she hurried on.

'I wrote to you, Vincenzo, and sent the letter to your apartment in Milan. I don't know why you didn't receive it but I definitely sent it.'

'Neither do I,' he began flatly, and then stopped.

'What?' Lowri demanded, because it was obvious that he had thought of something.

'I went to America that year—to Chicago—for six months.' He shrugged. 'I was contacted by the surgical team there and asked if I would be interested in taking part in their exchange programme and I agreed.'

'When was this?'

'The beginning of September. I remember stepping out of the airport and wondering if I'd made a mistake because it was pouring with rain!' He gave a little shudder then looked at her. 'When did you send your letter?'

'The end of August, not long after I found out I was pregnant,' Lowri told him and frowned. 'But even if my letter didn't arrive before you left, it should have been waiting for you when you got back.'

'Oh, I'm sure it would have been if a new concierge hadn't been hired while I was away. Apparently, a lot of post went missing while he was in charge of the building, most of it containing items of value. Your letter must have been one of the ones he threw away.'

'Good heavens!' Lowri exclaimed. 'That's awful.'

'It is. Thankfully, the police investigated following complaints by a number of residents and he was arrested, so he won't be doing it again. However, it doesn't make up for the fact that a lot of post went missing, your letter included, apparently.'

'It would explain it,' Lowri agreed slowly.

She bit her lip, mulling over what he had told her. For the past few years, she had assumed that he hadn't replied to her letter because he hadn't cared enough; however, it appeared that she had been wrong. The thought of having to adjust how she thought about him made her feel very on edge but she had to put it out of her mind for now. Right now she needed to find out what he intended to do and if she was right to think that he might agree to help her.

'I know that you probably need more time to think about it, but how do you feel about us having another child, Vincenzo? I wouldn't press you for an answer if it weren't so urgent.'

'I don't know how I feel. That's the honest answer.'

Vincenzo drew in his breath. Where was his legendary assurance when he needed it? He felt as keyed up as a teenager, his nerves so tightly strung that it was a wonder they didn't snap. He couldn't remember ever feeling this way before but, then, he had never been presented with this kind of a situation, had he? If he agreed to her request and they had another child, inevitably there would be consequences. How could he make her pregnant again and walk away? He would be tied to her, tied to the new baby as well as to their daughter, and the idea scared him.

He wasn't father material. He had no idea how to behave in that role. What if he ended up ruining his children's lives, albeit unwittingly? Everyone believed him to be cold and uncaring and what if they were right? What if he had buried his emotions so deep and for so long that he could never unearth them? Children needed time and love. And love was something he knew very little about.

Oh, his grandmother had loved him. Nonna had done her best to make up for his father's lack of interest and she had succeeded to a point too. However, since Nonna had died, Vincenzo knew that he had become more withdrawn, even colder with other people. That was why his marriage had failed. Even though he and Carla had entered into the arrangement with their eyes open, his inability to show any emotion had been one of the reasons why Carla had divorced him.

What if he couldn't find it in himself to treat his children with the warmth they had a right to expect? What if he was incapable of loving them as they deserved to be loved? He could remember only too well how much he had longed to hear his father speak to him with affection. It had never happened but it hadn't stopped him hoping that it would. What if he was the same? What if he was emotionally bankrupt too?

Vincenzo felt panic assail him and it was such a rare feeling that it hit him harder than it would have hit most people. He was out of his depth and he had no idea what to do to save himself.

Only this wasn't about him, was it? It was about a child. A little girl who could die if he refused to help her. His feelings didn't matter. His fears couldn't even *compare* to Lowri's.

He glanced at Lowri, his heart aching when he saw the lines that strain had etched on her face. She had been living with this nightmare for over a year, living with it and coping too. She must have her own doubts about what she had suggested but she had set them aside. She was prepared to have another baby with him if it meant she could save her daughter and yet here he was worrying about how he might feel and whether or not he would come up to the mark.

Vincenzo was suddenly filled with disgust at his own selfishness. Had he sunk so low that he was prepared to withhold the most precious gift of all, that of saving a life, to avoid having his own life disrupted?

'I'll do it.'

His voice sounded harsh in the softness of the summer day. All around them there were insects droning, bees buzzing, nature carrying on in its own gentle way. He saw Lowri turn, saw the question in her eyes, and knew he couldn't bear to hear her voice it out loud. If she asked him outright then he might just reconsider, allow cowardice to dictate his actions rather than compassion.

'I agree to us having another baby if there's a chance it will help Megan,' he said shortly, wanting to make it perfectly clear with the minimum fuss.

'I... Thank you.' Tears glimmered on her lashes and hung there like precious jewels.

Vincenzo turned and stared at the lake, needing to focus on something other than her tears, tears that he longed to wipe away. He couldn't afford to get emotionally involved. He had to remember that the only reason she was here was for the sake of their daughter. If it weren't for Megan she would never have contacted him and the thought stung, for some reason.

'I'm not sure exactly how we set about this. Obviously, there's the time factor to consider. I did some research and apparently the fresher the sample, the better our chances of it working.'

'Sample?' Vincenzo repeated, pushing the thought

aside. He saw her blush and frowned. 'I'm sorry but I'm not sure what you mean.'

'The sperm sample.' She took a quick breath. 'Naturally, you'll want to wait for the results of the DNA tests before we go ahead—I've brought everything you need with me so that won't be a problem. But we'll need to make arrangements for the sperm sample to be delivered to me.'

Vincenzo felt as though he had been struck dumb. It had never even crossed his mind that she had come here to ask him for a sample of his sperm! He cleared his throat, afraid that he would say something far too revealing. To let her know just how disappointed he felt that they wouldn't be sleeping together was out of the question!

'Of course. There's an excellent medical courier service we use at the hospital. I can make arrangements with them.'

'Oh. Right. That sounds ideal.' She took a package out of her bag and placed it on the table. 'There are DNA samples in there from Megan and from me as well. You just need to add yours and send it off. It shouldn't take long to get the results back.'

'No. The tests are fairly quick nowadays,' Vincenzo agreed flatly, still reeling from the thought of what was expected of him. He took a deep breath, realising that he was in danger of making too much of it. So Lowri didn't intend to sleep with him—so what? He should be relieved that he would be able to sidestep any unnecessary complications.

He stood up when she rose, wondering why he found the idea less appealing than he should have done. Getting involved with her was something he intended to avoid at all costs. It was going to be difficult enough to deal with the thought of being a father without adding anything else to the equation.

The thought steadied him, helped him regain some much-needed equilibrium, and he smiled coolly at her. 'I shall be in touch once the results are back. We can finalise the arrangements then.'

'Of course.' She held out her hand. 'I really appreciate this, Vincenzo. I know it's a lot to ask, especially in the circumstances, but it's Megan's best hope of making a full recovery and I'm truly grateful to you.'

Vincenzo took her hand, trying to ignore the rush of awareness that hit him as his fingers closed around hers. 'You don't need to thank me. It's enough to know that I may be able to help her.'

He released her hand, relieved to break the contact. He led the way to the door, pausing briefly to glance at her. 'How are you getting back to Garda? I assume you came here by taxi, so have you arranged to be collected?'

'I…ehem…no,' she admitted. 'Don't worry. I'm sure I'll be able to flag down a cab on the way.'

'I doubt it.' He sighed, suddenly anxious to bring the meeting to an end. It was a lot to take in and he needed time to think about what had happened and what it meant. His whole life was about to change and it was worrying to know that the future he had mapped out so carefully now wouldn't follow the route he had planned.

'I'll get my gardener to run you back,' he said curtly. He shook his head when she started to protest. 'No. I insist. If you'll wait here, I'll go and find him.'

Vincenzo didn't give her time to say anything else

as he strode out of the door. Alfredo was digging over a border but he stopped immediately when Vincenzo told him what he wanted him to do. Five minutes later the car was turning out of the drive but he knew it wasn't the end of the matter. It couldn't be when he had promised Lowri that he would help her.

A shiver ran down his spine and he turned away, wondering if he had made a mistake by giving her his word. There would be no going back on it now, no way that he could reconsider, and the thought filled him with such a mixture of emotions that his breath caught. If Lowri's plan worked then he would be the father of not one but two children this time next year.

It was midnight by the time Lowri's plane landed. The flight had been delayed and she was exhausted after the hours she had spent waiting around in Milan. Cerys was waiting when she came through customs, anxiously scanning the faces of all the passengers. She opened her arms and Lowri stepped into them, feeling relief pour through her as her sister enveloped her in a hug.

'So, how did it go?' Cerys demanded as she let her go.

'He agreed.' Lowri drummed up a smile, although her insides were churning as they had been doing ever since Vincenzo had told her his decision.

'Really? Wow!' Cerys sounded so shocked that Lowri laughed.

'I know. I was stunned too. It was such a long shot, wasn't it? I mean, he hardly knows me…' She trailed off, unable to continue as her throat closed up with a sudden attack of nerves.

'You hardly know him, either,' Cerys reminded her, leading the way to the car park. She zapped open the car doors then treated Lowri to an old-fashioned look. 'You are sure about this? I mean, it's a huge step to have another baby even when you're in a proper relationship and this is very different.'

'I know, but what choice do I have?' Lowri's eyes filled with tears. 'If I don't have this baby and something happens to Megan then I'll always wonder if I could have prevented it. I couldn't live with myself, Cerys, really I couldn't!'

'I know. Take no notice of me. You're doing the right thing, love, and I'll be with you every step of the way.'

Cerys gave her a smile then got into the car and after a moment Lowri got in as well. She knew her sister was simply concerned about her and she appreciated it, but she couldn't pretend that she didn't have her own doubts. Having a baby was a big decision for any woman and all the more so in this situation.

Even though there was a greater chance of a sibling being a match for Megan, it wasn't guaranteed. From the moment she had decided to approach Vincenzo, she had ruled out the idea of having the baby tested before it was born for the simple reason that she knew she could never abort it. To destroy one life to possibly save another was something she couldn't do so she was going to have to trust to luck that the baby would be a suitable donor.

Should she have made that clear to Vincenzo? she wondered suddenly. She would hate him to think that she had misled him and she made a note to mention it when they next spoke.

Her heart jolted because the next time they spoke, they would have to finalise the arrangements for the sperm donation. There simply wasn't time to delay if this was to work and yet it seemed so cold, so...so *emotionless* to conceive a child this way. She sighed. It was emotionless, though. Vincenzo had agreed to her proposal purely to help Megan, not because he wanted to have another child with *her*. Feelings didn't enter into it, neither hers nor his...if he had any.

Lowri closed her eyes, unsure why the idea made her feel so sad. She and Vincenzo were just two people who had met at a time when each had needed comfort. They had fulfilled a mutual need but that was all it had been. Oh, she had found him very attractive; she still did. But she hadn't been in love with him or him with her. And yet for some reason the thought of him living his life in an emotional wasteland hurt. Vincenzo deserved more than that. He deserved to be loved, deserved to be *in love* too.

Vincenzo drove to Milan the following day. He went straight to a lab he had used many times during the course of his work and arranged to have the DNA tests done. He was a valued client and they promised to get the results back to him within a couple of days.

He gave them his phone number then headed to his lawyer's office next. Although Lowri had rejected his offer of financial support for Megan, he intended to make arrangements anyway. He also needed to know what his position was with regard to the child, and if he had any rights as her father. Maybe he was putting the cart before the horse when he still didn't have proof that Megan was his daughter but he needed to clarify the situation. Hopefully, he would feel better once he knew exactly what he was dealing with.

He sighed as he parked the car outside the lawyer's office. He had spent a sleepless night thinking about what had happened and what he had agreed to do and he still wasn't sure if he had made the right decision. The thought of how it was going to affect his life wasn't easy to deal with. Having one child would be difficult enough to cope with and having a second would only double the problems.

He could only imagine the impact it was going to have on his life and yet what else could he have done? If Megan was his daughter—and he was sure that she was—then he owed it to her to do everything he could to help her. After all, she was his flesh and blood and she would carry on the Lombardi name after he died.

The thought of having an heir had never occurred to him before and yet Vincenzo felt a sudden rush of pleasure at the idea. Getting out of the car, he made his way into the building with a new spring in his step. The name of Lombardi wouldn't die out now, as he had always assumed; it would be carried on by his own children. It felt remarkably good to know that too.

Vincenzo decided to go into work the following day. The meeting with his lawyer had taken far longer than he had expected but he now had a much clearer idea of his position. The lawyer had been quite blunt as he had explained that Lowri held all the cards at the present moment. She was the child's mother and until he had proof that he was Megan's father, he would have to abide by her wishes. While he could make arrangements to set up a trust fund in Megan's name, he couldn't *force* Lowri to accept financial support from him if she refused to do so.

For a man like him, who was used to being in sole charge of his affairs, it was unsettling to realise how tenuous his position actually was. Hopefully, a visit to the hospital would help to put some much-needed balance back into his life.

The familiar smell of antiseptic greeted him as he stepped out of the lift and he inhaled deeply. He had missed this. Missed the smell. Missed the buzz. Missed the adrenaline rush that came from saving lives under the most difficult of circumstances. Neurosurgery was one of the most demanding specialities. It needed strong nerves and steady hands and he possessed both—or he had done until the skiing accident that had partially severed one of the major nerves in his arm.

Vincenzo flexed his fingers as he opened the scrub-room door. Although he was ninety-nine per cent certain that he had regained full use of his hand, there was still that tiny doubt, that one per cent of uncertainty. Until he was completely confident about his prowess, he wouldn't operate. He would use the time instead to sort out this business with Lowri and the baby.

Heat flowed through him at the thought of how he would like to sort it out and he paused, wanting to be in control when he saw his team. There was no point thinking that he would prefer it if they conceived this child the old-fashioned way; Lowri would never agree. However, he knew that it was one of the reasons why he hadn't been able to sleep. Every time he had closed his eyes his mind had conjured up pictures of them together. Although he had tried not to think about that night they had slept together, the memories had obviously lodged in his brain and all it had needed was an excuse to unleash them.

A shudder passed through him as he suddenly found himself recalling how smooth and silky her skin had felt when he had run his hands over it and how firm her breasts had been as he had caressed them...

A burst of laughter issuing from behind the partly opened door brought him back to the present and he frowned. He couldn't remember his team laughing like that; he would definitely have discouraged them if they had. He was about to enter the room and remonstrate with them when he heard someone speaking and recognised the voice as belonging to his second in command, Jack Wallace.

'Now, now, settle down, guys. You know our beloved leader wouldn't appreciate it if he thought we were having fun.' Jack's voice changed, his American drawl replaced by the parody of an Italian accent. 'The work we do here is far too serious to joke about.'

More laughter greeted this. Vincenzo felt a wave of embarrassment wash over him when he realised that they were laughing at *him* rather than at Jack's abysmal attempt to mimic him. He let the door swing shut, stunned that he should take any notice. What did it matter if he was a figure of fun? Why should he care if people thought he was too strict? He was a damned fine surgeon and he achieved the kind of results that most surgeons could only dream about. He didn't need their approbation or their love!

Swinging round, he made for the lift. Five minutes later he was in his car and heading back to his apartment. He parked in the underground garage then took the lift to the penthouse and let himself in. It took a mere ten minutes to pack himself a bag and that was it.

Glancing around the elegant, designer-styled rooms, he gave a dismissive shrug. There was nothing here he needed, nothing that he would miss either. They were merely *things*, purchased to create the right impression. He had no emotional attachment to anything in the apartment. No emotional attachment to anything in his life, in fact, and all of a sudden he hated it. Hated the apartment, hated the way he lived, although he had no idea what he planned to do about it.

Vincenzo picked up his case and left. He was going to take the first step towards changing his life and simply see where it led him.

CHAPTER FOUR

'SO THAT'S JUST about it. How's Megan? I bet she's thrilled to be home from hospital, isn't she?'

'Yes, she is.'

Lowri dredged up a smile, not wanting her co-worker Helen Graham to see that her comment had touched a nerve. Megan had been very tearful when Lowri had left her with Cerys that morning and she couldn't help feeling guilty. However, the nursing manager had been very good about letting her take time off while Megan had been in hospital and Lowri knew that she couldn't keep on expecting preferential treatment. It wasn't fair to the rest of the staff on the paediatric intensive care unit to have to cover for her.

'She's really excited because we're going to choose her a wig tonight when I get back from work.' Lowri laughed, trying not to think about the last time she had told this tale. She couldn't afford to think about Vincenzo and the plans they had made or she wouldn't be able to concentrate. 'Apparently, she wants a bright pink one, just like her favourite doll.'

'Good for her.' Helen laughed. 'I wouldn't mind a change of hair colour either, although my hubby would have a fit if I came back sporting bright pink locks. Hmm, might be a good enough reason to do it. He needs a bit of a shake up to stop him getting too complacent.'

Lowri laughed as Helen gave her a wink and left. Helen and her husband were about to celebrate their twenty-fifth wedding anniversary so whatever they were doing, it was obviously right.

She sighed as she picked up the patients' list. She hadn't even made it to the altar let alone started celebrating anniversaries. Although she'd had several relationships, none of them had worked out. When she had met Jonathan, she had honestly thought that she had found her ideal partner at last but look how wrong she had been. It made her wonder if she could trust her judgement even if she did meet someone else.

The thought reminded her of meeting Vincenzo and she frowned. She had never been the kind of woman who jumped into bed with a man at the drop of a hat so why had she slept with him? They had met by accident, literally, when he had bumped into her in the street.

Lowri had gone to Milan for a break, needing to get away from the situation she had found herself in. Discovering that Jonathan was married had been a massive shock. She might never have found out either if she hadn't answered his phone one day when he had been in the shower. She wasn't sure who had been the most surprised, herself or his wife as the poor woman had had no more idea what had been going on than Lowri had done.

When Jonathan had told her a short time later that he and his wife had separated and had begged her to take him back, Lowri had refused. He had tricked her, betrayed her, and all she had wanted was to put the whole unhappy episode behind her.

She had flown to Milan, intending to spend a few days there sightseeing before moving on to the Italian Lakes. She had been coming out of one of the more exclusive stores when Vincenzo had cannoned into her. He had been speaking on his phone at the time but he had immediately ended his call and insisted on taking her back into the store and buying her coffee.

Coffee had led to lunch and lunch to dinner at an exclusive little *trattoria* where the menu hadn't mentioned anything as vulgar as prices. Lowri had asked him to order for her, wary of choosing the most expensive dish, and when the food had arrived it had been superb. Whether it was because she had been in the mood to be reckless, but when he had asked to see her the following night, she had agreed.

They had got on so well together, she thought. There had been no uncomfortable gaps in the conversation, none of those uneasy pauses that could occur between strangers. He had told her he was a surgeon and had seemed pleased when she had explained that she was a senior sister on PICU. Whether that had created a bond between them, she wasn't sure, but talking to Vincenzo had been remarkably easy, the hours she had spent with him some of the happiest she could remember.

In a way, it was to be expected that they would end up in bed together, especially after he had told her about his divorce and she had told him about Jonathan's betrayal.

Lowri pulled herself up short. She was wasting time standing here thinking about all that. Taking the list with her, she started her rounds, reacquainting herself with her young charges. All the children in the unit were very ill. Some had been sent there following surgery, others had been admitted via A and E. Their needs were complex and varied and she focused solely on them as she went from bay to bay. Visiting hours were strictly regulated as the children needed to be kept quiet and there were no parents about apart from little Poppy Meadows's mum and dad.

Nine-year-old Poppy had been admitted following an RTA. She had been knocked down by a truck and suffered a serious head injury. She'd had a large blood clot removed from her skull and was being kept in a drug-induced coma which, hopefully, would allow her brain to heal. Now Mrs Meadows grabbed hold of Lowri's hand.

'How is she doing? I asked the other nurse but she said it was too early to tell.' The woman's voice caught. 'I'd much prefer to know the truth even if it isn't good news.'

'What Sister Graham told you was the truth,' Lowri explained gently. She patted Sarah Meadows's hand. 'We won't know anything more until Poppy wakes up, I'm afraid.'

'The consultant said there could be brain damage,' Adam Meadows put in dully. He looked at Lowri and she could see the plea in his eyes and understood. He wanted her to tell him that it wouldn't happen, that his little girl would be fine, but she couldn't do that, couldn't raise his hopes and maybe have to dash them. That would be too cruel, as she knew from experience.

'It's possible,' she said quietly, trying not to think about how she had clung to every shred of hope before Megan had been diagnosed with leukaemia. In her heart she had known that it was something serious but she had kept dreaming up new reasons for the bruises, the tiredness and repeated chest infections, and it had made it that much harder to face the truth. 'However, we won't know for sure until Poppy wakes up. All I can say is that you must try to remain positive. Poppy has come through the operation and that's something to hold onto.'

She patted Sarah's hand again then left the couple to sit with their daughter. Although some people claimed it was a load of nonsense, she firmly believed in the power of positive thought. Having both her parents here might be just what Poppy needed to help her pull through.

Lowri frowned. Would it have helped Megan if Vincenzo had been there when she'd been in hospital? she found herself wondering. She had never thought about it before; there had been no point. However, she found herself mulling over the idea as she went into the office. She had concentrated all her efforts on persuading Vincenzo to have another child but maybe it would also help Megan if he visited her?

She sighed, wondering how he would feel about the idea. He had made his views on fatherhood perfectly clear and there was no reason to think that he would agree to see Megan. Nevertheless, she decided that she would ask him anyway. He could only say no and if he did then she would have lost nothing.

Would she?

Lowri stilled. For some reason, she knew that she would feel deeply hurt if he rejected the idea of spending time with their daughter. In a funny kind of a way, it would feel as though he was rejecting her and what they had shared that night.

She bit her lip. Maybe they hadn't slept with each other out of love but there'd been something there, something deeper and more meaningful than mere sex.

Vincenzo checked into his hotel, although he didn't bother going up to his room. Leaving his bag with the concierge, he left again, nodding when the doorman asked if he needed a taxi. He gave the driver the address then sat back and watched the streets rushing past. He had never been to Liverpool before and he was surprised by how impressive the city was, the modern, high-rise towers sitting cheek by jowl with the famous Liver Building. The waterfront had been awarded World Heritage status and he could understand why because it really was spectacular.

He could happily live here, he decided, and was stunned by the thought and by the one that followed it: he could happily live here and spend time with his family.

Vincenzo closed his eyes, shutting out the view. He didn't want to be tempted into making a decision he would regret. His life was in Italy and it was madness to think of uprooting himself. There was too much tying him to his home country like his work, for instance, and... What?

His mind stalled. No matter how hard he tried, he couldn't think of another reason why he needed to remain in Italy. Although he had many acquaintances there, he had very few friends and most of them he saw only infrequently. They met for dinner or a drink once or twice a year at the most. They wouldn't really miss him if he moved away; he wouldn't miss them either and that seemed like the most damning indictment of all. There was no one on this earth that he would really and truly miss.

Except Lowri.

Vincenzo's eyes flew open, his heart racing as he stared out of the taxi window. He had barely spared Lowri a thought in the past five years so why in heaven's name did he imagine that he would miss her? And yet, deep down, in that place where his heart resided, he knew it was true. He would miss her if she disappeared from his life now, he would miss her an awful lot too.

Lowri was about to go for lunch when there was a crisis in PICU. Poppy Meadows's sats plummeted, setting off the alarm on her monitor. Lowri hurried to the bay. Amy Dempster, the staff nurse, was already there so Lowri asked her to escort Poppy's parents to the relatives' room. The last thing they needed was terrified parents getting in the way.

She placed an oxygen mask over Poppy's face but it didn't help very much. The child was still having problems breathing so as soon as Amy came back Lowri asked her to page Simon Rivers, the surgeon who had operated on the child. She sighed when Amy came back to tell her that Simon was in Theatre and couldn't leave his patient. How typical that this should happen when the consultant was unavailable.

'He's sending Cameron Howard instead,' Amy informed her, and grimaced. Cameron was one of the registrars and highly unpopular on the unit. He had an overbearing manner that didn't go down well with either the staff or patients.

'How long will he be?' Lowri asked, adopting a neutral expression. Cameron had become rather a nuisance lately. He had asked several of the single nurses out and she had a nasty feeling that she was next on his list, seeing as they had all refused. She sighed. She could only hope that he wouldn't start pestering her today. She had enough to cope with without thinking about dating him or anyone else.

The thought immediately reminded her of Vincenzo and she felt heat flow through her. As she checked Poppy's sats again, Lowri could feel her heart racing. As soon as the DNA results came back, they would have to proceed to the next stage in her plan. Whilst part of her wanted to get it over with as soon as possible, another part balked at the idea of what needed to be done. It seemed so *cold-blooded* to conceive this child through artificial insemination and yet what was the alternative? That she and Vincenzo should sleep together, turn what was in truth a practical solution to this problem into a romantic assignation?

Lowri snorted in disgust and saw Amy look at her in surprise. Fortunately, there was no time for the nurse to ask any questions because Cameron had arrived. He came striding into the unit, brimming over with self-importance.

'Problems?' he demanded, stopping by the bed.

Lowri quickly outlined what had happened, quashing the thought that he could see for himself what was going on if he cared to look. However, if Cameron enjoyed the feeling of power it gave him to have her explain, then so be it. He nodded when she finished, adopting his gravest expression, the one they all believed he practised in front of his mirror: brilliant young doctor graciously sparing the time to educate the minions.

'Hmm, it looks as though something has gone wrong. I'll need to send her for a scan, of course, before I can determine exactly what.'

'Of course,' Lowri agreed dryly, wondering if he honestly thought she hadn't worked that out for herself. 'I've phoned Radiology and they can fit her in right away.'

'Have you indeed?' Cameron didn't look happy about her taking the impetus from him. He frowned. 'It might be best to wait a while, see if her breathing settles down, rather than rush things.'

'I don't think we can afford to wait,' Lowri protested. She glanced at the monitor and shook her head. 'Her sats are already low and we don't want them dropping any further.'

'I shall be the judge of that, Sister Davies,' Cameron said repressively. He looked up when Donna Wilson, one of the newest additions to their staff, appeared. 'Yes? What is it, nurse? If you have a message for me then be quick about it. As you can see, I'm extremely busy.'

'I…um… It's not for you,' Donna said hurriedly. She turned to Lowri. 'There's a gentleman asking to speak to you, Lowri. He said it was urgent or I wouldn't have interrupted you.'

'Oh. Right. Did he give you a name?' Lowri asked, wondering who it could be, unless it was the parent of one of their young charges, of course.

'Lombardi...or at least I think that was what he said,' Donna told her, and blushed. 'I may have got it wrong, though. Sorry.'

'No, it's fine.' Lowri only just managed to stop herself blushing too. What was Vincenzo doing here? she wondered as she turned to Cameron. They'd already agreed that he would telephone her when he received the DNA results so it couldn't be that. What did he want? Unless he was having second thoughts and had come to tell that he wouldn't be going through with their plan after all.

The thought was more than she could bear. Ignoring the annoyance on Cameron's face, she tersely informed him that she would be back shortly and hurried to the office. Vincenzo was standing by the window when she went in and he turned when he heard her footsteps. Just for a moment his expression was unguarded and Lowri felt her breath catch. Why was he looking at her that way, as though he had never really *seen* her before? She had no idea what it meant and before she could attempt to work it out, the shutters came down again.

'I thought I should let you know that I was in England,' he said curtly, moving away from the window.

'I...ehem... So I can see.' Lowri took a quick breath and used it to chase away any more such fanciful notions. Vincenzo hadn't looked at her any differently from how he had looked at her when they had last met, she told herself firmly, yet, oddly, the reassurance had less effect than it should have done. In her heart she knew that something had changed.

'Is there a reason why you decided to come here?'

she said, refusing to dwell on the thought. What difference did it make how Vincenzo looked at her? Her only concern was that he hadn't changed his mind about them having this baby.

The thought brought a rush of heat to her face and she looked away, needing a moment to calm herself down. Every time she thought about what needed to happen if she was to have this child, she found herself shying away from it. However, she couldn't keep ignoring the facts, couldn't pretend that it was going to be an immaculate conception. She was going to have to impregnate herself with Vincenzo's sperm if this child was to be born.

'I decided it was time that I met Megan. Bearing in mind that you contacted me specifically to help her, I thought it only right.'

He gave a very Latin shrug, his shoulders moving lightly beneath his perfectly tailored jacket. He was wearing formal clothes that day—a dark grey suit teamed with a cream shirt and a grey and tan silk tie. He looked every inch the wealthy, sophisticated man she had met in Milan yet Lowri found herself thinking that she much preferred how he had looked when they had sat in the garden of the villa. He had seemed so much more approachable that day, less aloof. It had made it that much easier to understand why she had slept with him.

She drove that foolish thought from her head. Vincenzo had agreed to help her and she needed to be sure that he hadn't changed his mind. 'So you haven't had second thoughts?'

'Second thoughts?' he echoed, his dark brows rising steeply.

'About the baby. Because if you have, Vincenzo, then I'd much prefer it if you told me straight away rather than lead up to it.' She stared back at him, struggling to ignore the thunderous beating of her heart. If he had changed his mind, she had no idea what she was going to do, how she was *ever* going to help Megan.

'Of course not.' His tone was icy. 'I am not in the habit of going back on my word.'

'Then you must be a rare sort of a man indeed.' Lowri wasn't sure why she'd said that. After all, the last thing she should do was alienate him. Nevertheless, the words slid out before she could stop them and she saw him stiffen.

'Don't judge me by your past experiences. All men are not alike.'

'I'm sorry.' She gave a little shrug, knowing that she deserved the rebuke. 'I shouldn't have said that. I apologise.'

'No, you shouldn't. But maybe it's to be expected in light of what's happened.'

His tone softened, took on a seductive note that made her skin prickle with awareness. Lowri's breath caught as she felt it run through her, starting at the top of her head and working its way down to her toes, a sensation of light and heat and recognition that was all the more disturbing when she couldn't recall experiencing anything like it before. Her mind was still struggling to deal with what was happening when he continued.

'You haven't had an easy time in the past few years, Lowri, and it's understandable if your view of men is somewhat jaded. However, I can only repeat what

I told you before: I don't go back on my word. Ever.' His eyes held hers fast and she found it impossible to look away. 'I promised to give you another child and that's exactly what I shall do, although I've decided that we may need to alter our plan.'

'Alter our plan?' Lowri repeated uncertainly. Her heart began to race when she saw the way he was looking at her. It was hard to force out the question when she had a feeling that she wouldn't like the answer but she didn't have a choice. 'What do you mean?'

'Simply that artificial insemination isn't anywhere near as successful as the old-fashioned method.' His eyes held hers fast. 'If you are committed to having this child, Lowri, we need to sleep together. That will give you a much better chance of conceiving.'

CHAPTER FIVE

'SORRY ABOUT THE delay. I couldn't leave Theatre.'

Vincenzo swung round when a man suddenly appeared in the doorway. He heard Lowri take a deep breath and knew that she was as shocked by his suggestion as he was himself. He certainly hadn't planned on saying that! Definitely hadn't come here with the express intention of asking her to sleep with him. However, now that he had, he realised that it was what they needed to do.

Artificial insemination *was* nowhere near as effective as the natural method of conception. Although he couldn't quote the statistics, he knew for a fact that far too many things could go wrong and adversely affect the outcome. There simply wasn't time to waste if they hoped to help Megan so they needed to give themselves the best chance of succeeding. Even then Lowri might not get pregnant immediately. It could take several attempts before it happened. The thought made his blood heat. They might need to sleep together more than once.

Vincenzo drove that thought from his head as she turned to him. He didn't want her to know just how much the idea appealed to him. He couldn't afford to get too deeply involved with her, although how he was going to stop it happening in view of what he had suggested was anyone's guess.

'I'm sorry but I have to go,' she said flatly. 'Where are you staying?'

'One of those new hotels, near the Alfred Dock.'

'Albert.' She gave him a quick smile and his heart lifted when he saw the amusement in her eyes and realised he was responsible for it. 'It's Albert Dock, not Alfred.'

'Of course. My mistake. *Mi scusi!*'

Vincenzo smiled back, enjoying the fact that he could make her smile even at such a tense moment. It struck him all of a sudden that he wanted to do it again, wanted to watch her eyes light up and her mouth soften, wanted to see the strain melt from her face. He breathed in sharply, stunned that he should feel this way. When had someone else's feelings been so important to him? Why did he care if she was happy or sad? He couldn't explain it but he knew that he cared how she felt and that he cared an awful lot too.

'I hope I'm not speaking out of turn but are you Vincenzo Lombardi, by any chance?'

Vincenzo looked up when the other man addressed him, although it was an effort to drag his eyes as well as his thoughts away from Lowri. *'Sì.'*

'I thought so!' The man laughed as he stepped forward and held out his hand. 'Simon Rivers. I was lucky enough to hear a lecture you gave a couple of years ago about brain injuries. It was most enlightening, I can tell you.'

'Grazie.' Vincenzo shook his hand. 'I assume you have an interest in neurosurgery, Dr Rivers?'

'Very much so, although I'm not in your league.'
Simon turned to Lowri and smiled ruefully. 'Dr Lombardi is in a class of his own, although I'm sure I don't need to tell you that.'

The implication was only too clear. Vincenzo felt heat run through him when he realised that Simon believed he and Lowri were an item. He was about to correct him when one of the nurses came rushing into the office.

'Can you come, Lowri? Poppy's sats have dropped again.'

'Of course.'

Lowri hurried out of the door with Simon Rivers hard on her heels, and after a moment's hesitation Vincenzo followed them. They were already bent over the child when he reached the bed so he stood to one side and watched as they went through the familiar routine of checking her obs. He glanced at the monitor and frowned when he saw how low her oxygen levels were. The situation needed to be addressed urgently.

'It looks like another bleed,' Simon concluded. 'We need to get her into Theatre pronto.' He looked up. 'I don't suppose you'd care to observe, would you, Dr Lombardi? I would appreciate your advice.'

'Of course. I'd be honoured,' Vincenzo replied, and realised that he meant it too. It had been such a long time since he'd been in Theatre, far too long, in fact.

It was all systems go after that. Poppy was taken straight to Radiology and by the time they had scrubbed up, the results of the scan were up on the screen. Vincenzo nodded when Simon Rivers pointed to a darkened area that could only have been caused by another bleed. The area in question was worryingly close to the medulla, the part of the brain that relayed signals to the muscles involved in speech. It also contained groups of nerve cells involved in the regulation of heartbeat, breathing, blood pressure and digestion. Operating in this area was always nerve-racking as there was so much at stake.

Simon wasted no time. Vincenzo stood to one side, close enough to observe what was happening and yet not so close that he would get in the way. Simon worked swiftly and neatly and Vincenzo voiced his approval.

'*Bene*. It is good to have confidence in your own ability. You are less likely to make mistakes that way.'

'Thank you.'

Simon didn't labour the point but Vincenzo could tell he was pleased and was glad that he had complimented the younger man. It was something he wouldn't normally have done and he found himself making a note to do it in the future. People responded far more positively to praise than they did to criticism.

It was a rare insight into his past behaviour and Vincenzo knew that he would take it on board. Maybe he was too hard on his staff and needed to lighten up occasionally. If it meant they performed better under pressure then it would be worth loosening the reins a little.

The thought lingered as the operation ran its course. By the time Simon declared that he had done all he could, Vincenzo was feeling fairly confident about the outcome. He accompanied the younger man to the changing room, shaking his head when Simon expressed his doubts about what he had done.

'In my opinion, you did everything possible for

the child. Now it's a question of waiting to see what happens.' He shrugged. 'We can only do our best, Dr Rivers. No more than that.'

'I know.' Simon grimaced as he tossed his gown into the hamper. 'It's just that you always feel that you could have done more, don't you?'

'*Sì,*' Vincenzo agreed, somewhat surprised that he should make such an admission. He never voiced any doubts about what he had done. Even when he wasn't one hundred per cent confident about the outcome, he preferred to keep it to himself. Admitting that he had concerns seemed like an admission of failure and yet all of a sudden he was willing to concede that there had been times when he had felt that he hadn't quite come up to the mark.

'It's only natural. When you care about what you do—as we both do—you are bound to wonder if you could have gone that bit further, tried that bit harder. But we're only men, Dr Rivers. We can only do what we can and hope that it's enough.'

'You're right. I know you are. I just needed to be reminded.' Simon gave him a grateful smile and headed into the shower.

Vincenzo followed more slowly, wondering why he had opened up like that. He had never felt the need to do so before and he wasn't sure what had brought about such a change in his behaviour. Was it because he was feeling more emotional than usual? Allowing his feelings to surface rather than keeping them safely buried?

He sighed. He knew it was true and it was worrying to face the fact that he was no longer fully in control. He couldn't afford to relax his guard, especially now. He had to be able to take a step back, to distance himself if Lowri agreed to his suggestion about how they should conceive this baby. If he allowed himself to get emotionally involved, it would never work; *he* would never be able to walk away afterwards, as he had to do. After all, it wasn't him Lowri wanted but the child he could give her. He must never forget that.

Lowri got Poppy Meadows settled and then went to find the child's parents. Although Simon would speak to them shortly, she knew they would be anxious for news. They leapt to their feet when she opened the door to the relatives' room and she smiled reassuringly at them.

'Poppy's back from Theatre. Mr Rivers will fill you in on all the details but I thought you'd want to know that she's come through the operation.'

'Thank heavens!' Sarah Meadows sank down onto the couch and buried her face in her hands. Her voice was muffled when she continued. 'I so afraid that she...she...'

She couldn't go on but Lowri understood. She too had been in this position and knew how it felt to fear the worst. Sitting down beside Sarah, she gave her a hug.

'It's early days yet but she's a tough little thing, a real fighter, and that will go in her favour.'

She looked round when the door opened, feeling her heart jolt when she saw Vincenzo follow Simon into the room.

All of a sudden she wished he had been there when Megan had been so ill. Maybe it wouldn't have affected the outcome but it would have helped *her* to have him there. The thought startled her because she had never once considered contacting him. He had failed to reply to her letter informing him that she was pregnant so there had seemed no point. Now, however, the sense of loss she felt at not having been able to share the experience with him stunned her. Having a child who was critically ill brought people together, so was that what she would have wanted, to create a bond between them?

Lowri shook her head to dislodge the idea but it refused to budge. It settled into her mind and stayed there throughout the whole time that Simon was speaking to the Meadows. When he stood up to leave, Lowri shot to her feet, desperate to escape from a situation that was in danger of creating so much upheaval in her life. There was no bond between her and Vincenzo, neither did she want there to be. Especially not after what he had proposed earlier!

Lowri escorted the parents back to the unit and left them there. Simon had already left when she went back to the office but Vincenzo was still there. She paused in the doorway, wondering what she was going to do. Vincenzo was right—artificial insemination wasn't nearly as effective as the more usual way of conceiving a child. But could she do it, could she sleep with him again to save Megan?

'Dr Rivers is a very skilful surgeon. I was impressed by his work.'

Lowri started, only then realising that she had been standing there without uttering a word. Colour ran up her cheeks but she made herself meet Vincenzo's eyes. She couldn't allow her feelings to get in the way of what needed to be done. She had to concentrate on Megan and what it could mean for her if she gave birth to a child who proved to be a suitable match for her. How she felt about sleeping with Vincenzo was of very little importance compared to that.

'He's highly regarded by both the patients and the staff,' she agreed quietly. She took a quick breath, needing to get everything straight before her courage deserted her. 'How long do you plan on staying in England?'

'I haven't decided.' He gave a little shrug. 'There's nothing urgent at home that needs my attention.'

'But what about your work? Are you able to take time off without it causing a problem?' she persisted, trying to stem the nervous fluttering of her heart. If he wasn't planning to go back home once he had seen Megan then did it mean he was hoping to put his plan into action? The thought filled her with a rush of panic.

'I've been off work for the past six months so I'm sure they can manage without me for a while longer,' he said smoothly.

'Off work!' She exclaimed in surprise. 'Why? Have you been ill?'

He held up his right hand. 'I had a skiing accident earlier in the year and damaged a nerve in my arm. Thankfully, it appears to have healed but I need to be sure that I've regained full mobility in my hand before I return to Theatre.'

'I had no idea...'

She broke off because there was no reason why she should have known. They had led completely separate lives for the past five years and for some reason the thought made her feel even more nervous about what they were planning. Leaving aside the matter of how this baby was to be conceived, was it right to have another child when they had no intention of raising it together? Yet if they didn't go ahead, what would it mean for Megan? This was the best chance of providing a suitable donor for her, possibly the only chance.

'There's no reason why you should have known,' Vincenzo stated coolly, and for some reason Lowri found herself taking exception to the lack of emotion in his voice.

'No. I'd served my purpose, hadn't I? I doubt if you gave me much thought after that night.'

'I doubt if you thought about me very much either,' Vincenzo countered. His expression darkened. 'Did it never occur to you that your letter might have gone astray when I didn't reply?'

'No.' She shrugged, refusing to allow him to make her feel guilty. 'I naturally assumed you weren't interested.'

'So you never considered writing to me again?' His tone was harsher than ever and she glared at him.

'No. I didn't. We had an affair, Vincenzo. A holiday romance, if you prefer to call it that, like thousands of people do each year.' She gave a little laugh, hearing the bitterness it held but unable to do anything about it. Maybe she hadn't expected him to be delighted by the news that she was pregnant but his apparent lack of interest had hurt. Now all the old pain came bubbling to the surface. 'We didn't swear undying love to each other. We just slept together!'

'Oh, sorry. I'll come back later.'

Lowri spun round when she heard Amy's voice but the nurse had already hurried away. She sighed because the last thing she wanted was people talking about her. She had told no one the identity of Megan's father apart from Cerys, of course, preferring to keep it to herself rather than become the subject of yet more gossip. She'd had her fill of that when folk had found out about Jonathan so whenever anyone had asked her about Megan's father, she had told them simply that they were no longer together. Now she couldn't help wondering how long it would be before everyone knew that Megan was the result of a holiday fling.

She bit back a groan as an even worse thought struck her. She could just imagine what people were going to think if she got pregnant again!

Vincenzo unpacked his case and then took a shower. Wrapping himself in one of the towelling robes he found hanging behind the bathroom door, he went back to the bedroom. The evening stretched before him and he had no idea what he was going to do to pass the time. He had intended to invite Lowri out for dinner but it hadn't seemed like such a good idea in the end. She'd seemed very upset at the thought of the other nurse overhearing their conversation and he couldn't help wondering why. Was she ashamed of the circumstances that had led to Megan's birth?

He sighed. He had never thought about the impact it must have had on her life to find herself pregnant by a man she barely knew. It must have made the situation all the more difficult for her and he couldn't help wondering why she had decided to keep the baby. Lowri could have had the pregnancy terminated and he would have known nothing about it. Was that what he would have preferred?

He sat down on the bed, trying to work out how he felt. He had never wanted children yet the thought that Megan might never have been born hurt. It tugged at emotions he hadn't known he possessed, struck deep into a place he had never visited before. He had never met the child, had only seen photographs of her, and yet he realised with surprise that he cared about her. He *genuinely* cared.

The sudden trilling of his mobile phone cut through his musings. Vincenzo picked it up, his heart hammering when he recognised the number as that of the lab where he had taken the DNA samples. 'Lombardi,' he said curtly, holding his breath as the caller identified himself and then gave him the results. *'Grazie,'* he murmured before he broke the connection.

Tossing the phone onto the bed, he went to the window and stared out across the steel-grey waters of the river Mersey. The tests had confirmed that he was indeed Megan's father and although it was only what he had expected, it still came as a shock. Closing his eyes, he let the full import of what he had heard sink in.

He was a father. He had a child, a little girl who desperately needed his help if she was to survive. All of a sudden, Vincenzo realised that nothing mattered more than that, that it made no difference how hard it was for him: Megan's needs took precedence. Maybe he hadn't planned on being a father but that's what he was and what he intended to be too—with or without Lowri's approval.

His mouth thinned as he moved away from the window and started to dress. He had a feeling that Lowri wouldn't be happy about the idea of him playing an active role in his daughter's life but there was nothing he could do about it. He intended to be a proper father to their daughter and a proper father to this new baby they were planning to have as well. They were his flesh and blood, they carried his genes and he would make sure they bore his name too!

Lowri had just got Megan settled in front of the television when the doorbell rang. Leaving the sitting-room door ajar, she went to answer it. Megan had been very fretful since she had brought her home from Cerys's house and Lowri wasn't sure what was wrong with her. Not even the prospect of choosing the much-anticipated wig had cheered her up.

Her heart caught as she unlocked the front door. The consultant had warned her about the need to be on her guard. Megan was highly susceptible to any kind of infection at the present moment and she could only pray that it wasn't that. It would be too cruel if Megan ended up back in hospital when she had only just been allowed to come home.

'*Buona sera*, Lowri.'

Lowri started when she found Vincenzo standing on the step. 'What are you doing here?' she demanded, her tone less welcoming than it might have been. However, bearing in mind what had happened earlier in the day, she felt she could be forgiven for not welcoming him with open arms.

'I came to see you. And Megan, of course.'

His tone was bland yet Lowri sensed a certain nuance in it that made her heart race. She had a feeling that there was more to this visit than he was prepared to admit and it was unsettling not to know what exactly was going on.

'Now really isn't a good time, Vincenzo,' she began, then stopped when a small voice piped up.

'Who is it, Mummy? Is it the lady with my wig?'

Lowri turned, her heart aching when she saw her daughter standing behind her. Even though Megan had lost all her hair during her treatment, the resemblance between her and Vincenzo was so marked that it was impossible not to tell that she was his daughter. Vincenzo must have noticed it too because she heard him draw in his breath.

Lowri glanced at him, feeling tears spring to her eyes when she saw the expression on his face. That he was deeply moved by his first sight of their child wasn't in doubt and something inside her seemed to open up at the thought. For five long years she had tried her best to blank out the memory of that night. Now she realised that it would be impossible not to think about it.

She and Vincenzo had made love that night and by doing so they had created this precious child, a child who desperately needed their help if she was to survive. While she had always been prepared to do whatever was necessary to save Megan, she had never expected that Vincenzo would feel the same.

She bit her lip as a wave of panic washed over her. Maybe the situation hadn't changed; maybe it was still the same in many ways. However, knowing that Vincenzo cared what happened to Megan made a world of difference to how she felt about him. If she did agree to his proposal then making love again with Vincenzo wouldn't be merely a means to an end. It would be so much more.

CHAPTER SIX

'You look beautiful, *tesoro*.'

Vincenzo smiled at the little girl, surprised by how easily the endearment had slid from his lips. He had expected to feel awkward around her, ill at ease even. After all, he'd had very little to do with any children apart from during the course of his work. However, it was proving surprisingly easy to relate to her. Despite the fact that Megan was still rather fragile following her treatment, she had an innate sense of fun, which he found truly delightful. Now he tugged playfully on a bright pink strand of the wig she had chosen.

'You look like a *real* princess now.'

Megan laughed happily as she picked up the mirror and studied her reflection again. Vincenzo sighed as he watched her admiring herself. Maybe pink wasn't the obvious colour to have chosen but it seemed to have made her extremely happy and that was all that mattered.

'She really loves it, doesn't she?'

He glanced round when Lowri came back from seeing the wig fitter out, his heart aching when he saw the expression on her face. She had been through so much in the past year and it was understandable if she found this a highly emotional moment. Without pausing to think, he reached out and squeezed her hand.

'*Sì*. It may not be the colour we would have chosen but it makes her happy and that's what counts most, isn't it?'

'It is.' Tears welled in her eyes. 'There was a point when I didn't think I'd ever hear her laugh like that again.'

'It must have been horrendous for you,' he said gruffly. He wasn't used to dealing with all the emotions that were swirling around inside him and he found it hard to achieve the right balance, if he was honest. He rarely allowed himself to empathise with other people yet it was proving impossible to remain detached in this instance. After all, this was his daughter they were discussing and that made a world of difference, as he had discovered.

'It was. But it was much worse for Megan.'

She took a shuddery breath and withdrew her hand. Vincenzo managed to curb the urge he felt to reach for it again, only for his own benefit this time. He had no right to expect sympathy from her, no right to expect anything at all. Lowri had been through one of the worst experiences any parent could go through and she'd had to go through it on her own.

Maybe he wasn't to blame when he hadn't known that he had a child yet he couldn't help feeling guilty. It made him see that the decision he had made to be a proper father to Megan and the new baby had been the right one. He couldn't simply walk away, couldn't leave Lowri to cope on her own—it wouldn't be right. Now all he had to do was to convince her.

Vincenzo's heart sank at the thought. He didn't say

anything as Lowri excused herself and took Megan up to bed. How could he convince her that he was to be trusted? How could he make her understand that he genuinely wanted to help? They knew so little about each other and it was only natural that she should be wary of his motives.

Maybe they didn't know a lot about each other but there had been a real connection between them that night they had made love.

His breath caught as the truth hit him squarely in the chest. He had felt things for Lowri that night that he had never felt for any woman, including his ex-wife. That was why he had gone to such lengths to forget about her afterwards. He had been afraid of what it had meant, afraid of all the feelings she had aroused and where they could lead.

He frowned. How did he feel about her now? He tried to work it out but it was impossible to make sense of all the emotions that were whirling around inside him and he sighed. It was more important than ever that he understand exactly what he was dealing with. Once he announced his decision to play a role in Megan's life there would be no going back. He would have to keep his word no matter what happened between him and Lowri.

Lowri closed the bedroom door then waited for a moment to make sure that Megan really was asleep. She sighed as she made her way downstairs. All the excitement had worn her out and she could only hope that it hadn't been too much for her. She didn't want anything to hinder her recovery, to set her back. She wanted Megan to regain her strength because it would help when she underwent the stem-cell transplant.

Lowri bit her lip as she stepped off the last tread. She was putting the cart before the horse because there was no chance of Megan having the transplant unless a suitable donor was found. It made it all the more imperative that she and Vincenzo carry out their plan and yet she felt more nervous than ever about it. Something had changed. *Vincenzo* had changed. And she was no longer sure what she was dealing with.

She squared her shoulders as she opened the sitting-room door. Even if the situation had changed in some way, the fact remained that Megan's best chance of making a full recovery was by undergoing a transplant. The sooner she and Vincenzo made a start on making it happen, the better.

'Is she asleep?'

'Yes.' Lowri shrugged with feigned nonchalance. She had never expected Vincenzo to visit her and to have him here in her home made her feel very on edge, especially in view of what he had suggested earlier about them sleeping together. The thought sent a rush of heat through her and she hurried on. 'She took longer to settle than usual because of all the excitement, I expect.'

'Choosing the wig obviously meant a lot to her,' he agreed with a smile that tugged at her heartstrings in a way she didn't welcome.

She didn't want to feel any kind of connection to him. Certainly didn't want to get emotionally involved with him. When Vincenzo returned to Italy, she didn't want to be left with regrets. She just wanted to be pregnant with his child!

The thought was too much to deal with and she jumped to her feet. 'Would you like a drink? I've a bottle of wine in the fridge if you'd care for a glass.'

'*Grazie*. That would be very nice. We shall be able to celebrate the news I received earlier this evening.'

'Oh. What news was that?' Lowri asked uncertainly.

'The DNA results have confirmed that I am Megan's father. That is something to celebrate, *si*?'

'I...ehem. Yes, it is.'

Lowri dredged up a smile before she hurried from the room. She took the wine out of the fridge then took a deep breath. Now that they had proof of Vincenzo's paternity, it was time to get down to the nitty-gritty and work out exactly when they were going to sleep together. Vincenzo was right, of course, because there was a far better chance of them conceiving a child naturally. Time was of the essence and she had to set aside any doubts she had and agree. Even so, she might not get pregnant straight away; it could take more than the one attempt, in fact.

Lowri groaned as she put the bottle and the glasses on a tray. That was something else she needed to think about. How many attempts would it take for her to get pregnant? And was she prepared to sleep with Vincenzo not just once but possibly several times?

Her hands were shaking as she carried the tray into the sitting room and set it down on the old toy chest that doubled as a coffee table. Picking up one of the glasses, she filled it with wine then handed it to Vincenzo and sat down before her legs gave way. It could take *months* before she got pregnant, dozens of occasions when she would need to sleep with him. Even if she ignored the logistics of making it happen, with her living in England and him living in Italy, was she really prepared for that?

'What's wrong?' His voice was low but Lowri heard the concern it held. It surprised her so much that she found herself blurting out the truth.

'I may not get pregnant straight away even if we do opt for the more natural method of conceiving.'

'Of course. These things rarely happen on demand, or so I'm led to believe.' His smile was cool but the awareness in his eyes filled her with heat. 'We may need to sleep together more than once, Lowri.'

'I…I just realised that.'

Lowri bit her lip, terrified that she would say something far too revealing. The thought of sleeping with Vincenzo again and again made her feel very odd. It would be that much harder to erase him from her life afterwards. That much more difficult to forget him and yet that was what she would have to do. Once they had achieved their objective, he would return to his world and she would remain here; their paths wouldn't cross again. The thought was oddly distressing.

'If you have any doubts about this then say so, Lowri. I wouldn't want you to go ahead and regret it later.'

The harsh note in his voice made her eyes fly to his face and she was shocked by the hurt she saw there. Vincenzo was always so cool and aloof that she hadn't imagined her unease would have an effect on him but it obviously had. She hurried to speak, wanting to reassure him that she still believed it was the right thing to do, but he beat her to it.

'I know we aren't in love with one another but we

have a child and we both want to do what's best for her. However, it would be intolerable to carry out this plan if one of us has misgivings. If you've changed your mind, Lowri, say so.'

'I haven't,' she began, then stopped. All of a sudden, she knew that she couldn't lie. It wouldn't be fair to him or to this child she hoped to conceive. 'It's not that I've changed my mind exactly. It's just that I never really thought about what it might entail.'

'You mean us having to sleep together,' he said bluntly, and she flushed.

'Yes.' She gave a little shrug. 'I thought it would be easier if we used artificial insemination. After all, I had no idea if you were in a relationship and it didn't seem right to create problems for you.'

'I'm not in a relationship, so there's no need to worry about that, I assure you.'

'No.' Lowri grimaced. 'However, it doesn't alter the fact that I hadn't expected this. It's…well, it's a lot to think about, quite frankly.'

'Especially when you have no idea how long it will take before you get pregnant?'

His tone was bland yet Lowri could feel her heart thumping. She sensed that her answer was important to him even though she wasn't sure why. Vincenzo had agreed to have this child because it could help Megan. As a doctor, it was important to him to do whatever he could to help save a life. However, she doubted if he was emotionally engaged in any way. The thought steadied her.

'I suppose so, although I have no intention of allowing that to stop me.' She looked him straight in the eyes, praying that he couldn't tell how nervous she felt. However, the last thing she wanted was him backing out because he thought she had developed cold feet.

'If it takes one attempt or a dozen, Vincenzo, I still want to go ahead. This baby is Megan's best hope of being cured and I'll do *anything* to make that happen!'

Vincenzo picked up his glass and took a mouthful of the wine, hoping it wouldn't choke him. He knew he was being ridiculous but it hurt to know that Lowri viewed making love with him on a par with some sort of highly distasteful experience.

He put down the glass, recalling how she had responded to him that night in Milan. She hadn't appeared to find his lovemaking distasteful then, he thought bitterly. Far from it. She had been as eager for his touch as he could have wished. He was used to women who thought like he did, women who viewed sex as just another physical need, an appetite that needed satisfying at regular intervals. Lowri's response had been very different, though.

She had given herself to him with a generosity that still surprised him even now when he thought about it. She hadn't tried to disguise her feelings, certainly hadn't feigned a world-weary cynicism like so many of the women he had slept with had done. She had responded with an honesty and a passion that had stunned him at first and delighted him later.

As for him, well, he had responded very differently to her too. For the first time ever, he realised, he had completely let go. He had forgotten that he was a top-flight surgeon, ignored the fact that his family had held a position of power for hundreds of years.

He had been simply a man making love to a woman he had wanted: a woman who had wanted him too.

'Have you eaten yet?'

His head spun as thoughts whirled around inside it, so that it was a moment before he realised that Lowri was waiting for him to answer. He cleared his throat, struggling to control the alarm he felt. He had wanted Lowri that night, wanted her more than he had wanted any woman before or since. It was little wonder that he felt so confused.

'No. It was too early for dinner when I left my hotel.' He gave a little shrug, affecting an insouciance he wished he felt. However, he refused to let her know how disturbed he felt. He didn't want anyone to have that kind of power over him, to influence his thoughts as well as his feelings. Like Lowri did.

'In that case would you like to eat with me?'

She treated him to a smile but he could tell how nervous she was and it helped him get a grip. Maybe he had wanted her that night but it was all in the past and it was what happened from here on that mattered more. Maybe they *were* going to make love; however, it wouldn't be the result of their desire for one another but because of their need to help their daughter. The thought steadied him.

'That is very kind of you. I would be delighted to eat with you so long as it isn't any trouble.'

'It isn't,' she assured him, standing up. She smoothed down the lightweight sweater she was wearing with a pair of well-worn jeans, immediately drawing his attention to the swell of her breasts and the curve of her hips.

Vincenzo sucked in his breath when he felt his

body respond in time-honoured fashion. He couldn't afford to start noticing things like that, he told himself sternly as she left the room. He had to remain detached, disinterested even when they set about creating this baby.

He groaned. How on earth could he remain detached when he was going to make love to her, when every curve, every dip and every hollow would be his to explore and caress?

He closed his eyes, trying to block out the pictures that filled his head but it merely brought them into even sharper focus. He could recall every centimetre of her body in exquisite detail, from the lush curves of her breasts to the erotic delicacy of her ankles. Her hair had been longer then, falling past her shoulders in a curtain of pale brown and gold. His hands clenched as he recalled its softness as he had threaded it through his fingers and pulled back her head so that he could skim kisses down her throat...

His eyes shot open and he made himself breathe deeply. In and out, half a dozen times, and then half a dozen more. He had to stop thinking about that night. It had been a one-off and it wouldn't be like that again. The first time they had made love he had just finalised his divorce and although he hadn't loved Carla, the ending of their marriage had affected him. It had seemed to highlight the emptiness of his life and he had felt very low afterwards.

As for Lowri, well, she had been through an equally traumatic experience. She had told him about her ex and Vincenzo had understood how hurt she must have felt. Was that why there had been that instant rapport between them? A feeling that they had found the one person who would understand?

He tried to convince himself that it was the key to what had happened, that it explained why making love with her had been so different, so intense. However, deep down, he sensed there had been more to it than that, a lot more.

He took another breath, held it until his vision blurred, until he couldn't see anything and especially not those intimate and disturbing pictures. Deep inside he knew that if he allowed that thought to take hold, he would regret it. He and Lowri had met at a time in their lives when they had both needed support and solace and that was all it had amounted to. To imagine it had been more than that would be a mistake. For both of them.

Lowri placed the plates on the table then checked that she had set out everything they needed. She'd grilled some salmon steaks and served them with new potatoes and a green salad. There was fresh fruit for pudding and coffee after that...

She bit her lip, realising that she was employing delaying tactics to put off the moment when she would call Vincenzo through to the kitchen. She wasn't sure what had happened before but there had been something going on, a sort of buzz that had made her feel very on edge.

She'd been thinking about that night in Milan but she had to forget about that and concentrate on what needed to be done. Maybe it had been wonderful and maybe Vincenzo had exceeded all her expectations as a lover but it didn't mean she was going to feel the same way when they made love again.

She huffed out her breath as she went to tell him that dinner was ready. Quite frankly, the sooner she got pregnant, the better. Then she and Vincenzo could get back to normal. Poking her head round the sitting-room door, she smiled politely at him. 'Dinner's on the table. I hope you like fish.'

'I do, very much, in fact.'

He stood up, smiling calmly as he walked to the door. He had shed his jacket and rolled up the sleeves of his shirt and she felt her heart lurch when she saw how dark his skin looked against the white cotton fabric. His whole body had been deeply tanned, she recalled as she led the way. Apart from a narrow strip around his hips...

'More wine?' She picked up the bottle, determined to drive the images from her mind. They would serve no purpose, only make it even more stressful when they did make love. Last time they had needed each other but it would be very different the next time it happened. They would be making love for Megan's sake, not for theirs.

'*Sì. Grazie.*'

Lowri shuddered when he replied in Italian. Although Vincenzo's English was excellent, several times that night he had slipped back into his mother tongue and the sound of his deep voice was yet another reminder she didn't need. She filled his glass then sat down, determined to channel her thoughts along the direction they needed to take.

She mustn't make the mistake of thinking that what she had felt that night was what she would feel again.

She had been in a bad place at the time and Vincenzo had helped her through it. That was why their love-making had seemed so intense.

They ate in silence. Lowri couldn't think of anything to say and it appeared that Vincenzo felt the same. He placed his cutlery neatly on his plate after he had finished and smiled at her.

'That was delicious, Lowri. Thank you.'

'You're very welcome.' She gathered together their plates and stood up. 'I'm afraid there's only fruit for pudding.'

'Not for me, thank you. I've had more than enough.' He looked up and she felt her breath catch. It was obvious that he was going to say something and all of a sudden she didn't want to hear it. Picking up the plates, she took them to the sink and turned on the taps.

'How about coffee, then?' she asked, her nerves humming with tension when she glanced round and discovered that he was standing up.

'No coffee for me, either,' he replied quietly, as he came to stand behind her.

'Oh, right. Well, I think I'll have a cup.' Lowri reached for the kettle but he placed his hand on her arm.

'Can it wait? It seems to me that we have something far more pressing to think about than coffee.'

His deep voice grated and Lowri felt the tiny hairs all over her skin spring to attention. When he turned her round to face him, she didn't protest, couldn't even attempt to do so when she found it impossible to speak. Bending, he looked into her eyes, his own eyes as deep and as fathomless as the night.

'You explained how urgent it is that Megan have this transplant so maybe we should be concentrating on making that happen?'

CHAPTER SEVEN

'I…I DON'T think we should rush things. Why don't we make arrangements to meet another night?'

Vincenzo heard the panic in Lowri's voice and sighed inwardly. Maybe he should have given her more warning rather than spring it on her like that, although it shouldn't be that much of a surprise to her. After all, *she* had stressed the urgency of the situation when she had sought his help, hadn't she? No, if she was employing delaying tactics, it was because the idea of making love with him wasn't a particularly pleasant one.

It was hard to hide his chagrin but he knew that it wouldn't achieve anything to make an issue of it. He summoned a smile, wanting to make the occasion as stress-free as possible for both of them. 'If that's what you would prefer then that's what we shall do.'

'Thank you.' She smiled thinly as she stepped away from him. 'I expect we shall both feel better if we know exactly when and where it's going to happen.'

'I expect you're right,' he agreed, struggling to keep the irony out of his voice. He shrugged. 'I wonder how many other couples have found themselves in this position?'

'I've no idea but there are bound to be some,' she said, her voice quavering. She looked up and he could see the uncertainty in her hazel eyes. 'It is the right thing to do, isn't it, Vincenzo?'

'From what you have told me, and what I have read for myself, it's the only thing we can do if we want to help Megan.'

'But what if we have another child and it isn't a suitable match? We'll have gone through all this for nothing!'

'That is something only you can decide.' He caught hold of her hands. 'Are you willing to take that risk, Lowri?'

'I think so,' she murmured, staring up at him.

'Bene.'

He pulled her to him, feeling the shudder that passed through her when their bodies came into contact. He bit back a sigh, aware that it wasn't passion that had caused her to react that way. The thought of what they needed to do scared her and in that second he realised that his feelings didn't matter. He wanted to make this as easy as possible for *her.*

He cupped her face between his hands, over-whelmed by the thought. He had never experienced this need to protect someone else before. The lack of compassion he had been shown as a child meant that he rarely considered other people's feelings, but this was different. This was Lowri. And how she felt mattered to him.

His mind reeled as he tried to absorb that thought but it was just too big. Too complex. Too scary. He thrust it away as he covered her mouth with his. He wasn't sure why he felt such an overpowering desire to make physical contact with her but he needed to feel her mouth under his, *needed* this connection!

There was a moment when he sensed her start to pull away and he steeled himself for the impending rejection, but then the next second she was kissing him back. Vincenzo groaned when he felt her lips mould themselves to his because it wasn't what he had expected. He had thought after her initial reaction that he would have to woo her, seduce her even, but it appeared that she didn't need seducing after all.

The thought filled him with such intense pleasure that he gasped. He felt her tense and ran his hands down her back to soothe her. When he drew her closer, she didn't resist and his heart swelled with a mix of emotions he had never experienced before. It struck him then that when they did make love it was going to change his life. He wouldn't be the same person he had been after he had made love to Lowri again.

Lowri could feel her heart racing. She had never expected to feel this way but it appeared she was as powerless to resist Vincenzo's kisses now as she had been five years ago. Heat scorched along her veins when she felt his hands run down her spine. Everywhere his fingers touched she could feel ripples of sensation erupt. It was as though her skin was on fire, flames licking and dancing across its surface.

All thoughts about waiting seemed to have disappeared from her mind. When his hand came to rest on her bottom, she held her breath, waiting for the moment when he would urge her closer.

'*Mummy!*'

The cry from upstairs broke the spell. Lowri

wriggled out of Vincenzo's arms and ran to the door. Megan was standing on the landing when she reached the bottom of the stairs and it was immediately obvious that she had been sick. Lowri ran upstairs and scooped her up into her arms.

'It's all right, darling. Mummy's here.'

'I've been sick,' Megan wailed, pressing her face into the crook of Lowri's neck.

'Shh, it doesn't matter.' Lowri felt fear envelop her when she discovered how hot Megan felt. She carried her back into the bedroom and sat her down on the bed then went to fetch the thermometer from the bathroom cabinet. Vincenzo was kneeling beside the bed when she went back and she frowned.

'You don't need to stay. We'll be fine.'

'I want to stay.' He looked up and she realised that it was pointless arguing when she saw the grim determination in his eyes.

She shrugged as she placed the thermometer under Megan's tongue.

'As you wish.'

Vincenzo didn't say anything else as he knelt beside the bed, holding Megan's hand. It seemed to take for ever before the thermometer beeped. Lowri's heart sank when she checked the display. Megan's temperature was far higher than it should have been, which could only mean that she had contracted some sort of an infection.

Vincenzo took the thermometer from her and frowned. 'It's very high. Did the consultant give you instructions on what to do if this happened?'

'Yes. He said I was to phone the hospital and make arrangements for Megan to be seen immediately,'

Lowri explained. She lowered her voice. 'She's going to be so upset if they keep her in again.'

'Let's face that if and when it's necessary,' Vincenzo said firmly. He turned and smiled at the little girl. 'So, *tesoro*, it seems that you need to go to the hospital. Why don't you tell me which of your toys you want to take with you while Mummy phones the doctor? Would Teddy like to go? Or how about this rabbit? Maybe he'd like to go and meet all the nurses.'

'She's a girl rabbit,' Megan told him importantly. 'She's called Rosie.'

'Ah. *Mi scusi!* I should have realised she was a girl rabbit because she has a lovely pink ribbon around her neck.'

He pulled a wry face, which made Megan laugh. Lowri's heart lightened a little as she went to make the call because it seemed like a positive sign. She spoke to the ward sister and, as expected, she was told to take Megan in straight away. Vincenzo stayed while she washed and changed Megan then packed her a bag, and she was glad of his help. Not only was he remarkably good at distracting Megan, but it helped her to have him there.

She sighed as she slipped a clean nightdress into the case. She mustn't get too used to having him around, though. Vincenzo had made it clear that he didn't intend to play an active role in Megan's life and it would be foolish to come to rely on him. She must never forget that when he returned home, there'd be just her and Megan, plus possibly another baby in a few months' time.

Lowri bit her lip as the full enormity of her situation hit her. She would be the mother of two small

children, one of whom was seriously ill. It was going
to be a lot to cope with on her own.

'We'll start her on broad-spec antibiotics if her temperature doesn't drop soon, although it could turn out
to be something and nothing. These spikes in temperature do occur occasionally following chemotherapy.'

Vincenzo listened attentively as the consultant,
Alistair Simpson, outlined Megan's treatment plan.
It was after midnight and Megan was fast asleep in
a side room leading off the main ward. Although her
temperature had fallen slightly, it was still higher than
it should have been and he agreed with the other man's
decision to keep her in.

'How long do you plan to keep her here?'

Vincenzo glanced round when Lowri spoke, sighing when he saw how exhausted she looked. That this
new setback had caused her a great deal of stress was
obvious. Reaching out, he covered her hand with his,
wanting to offer her whatever comfort he could.

'I'm afraid I can't tell you that.' Alistair Simpson
grimaced. 'If it does turn out that Megan has contracted an infection then we need to make sure it's
cleared up before she can return home. In her weakened state even the most innocuous childhood illness
can have a devastating effect.'

'Of course.'

Lowri dredged up a smile but Vincenzo could tell
how upset she was. The fact that Megan had needed
to be readmitted to hospital so soon after she had
been allowed home must be extremely worrying for
her. He frowned as an idea suddenly occurred to him.

'There would be less chance of Megan contracting an infection again if she didn't come into contact with any other children,' he suggested.

'Of course,' Alistair agreed. 'The more contact she has with other children, the greater the risk of her catching something. Normally, her immune system would help her fight off most illnesses but the drugs she's received have weakened her body's defences. That's why we advise parents to keep their children away from anyone who's got a cough or a cold or something similar.'

'She will improve, though,' Vincenzo clarified, more for Lowri's benefit than his own. He understood the situation perfectly and agreed wholeheartedly with Alistair's decision to keep Megan in hospital. He would have done the same thing himself, in fact, but he simply couldn't bear to see Lowri looking so despondent.

'Oh, yes. Her immune system will improve but it'll take some time,' Alistair warned. 'That's why it's essential that you take all possible precautions in the meantime.'

'Of course.' Vincenzo realised they had come to the end of the consultation. He stood up and held out his hand. 'Thank you, Dr Simpson. I appreciate the fact that you came in after hours to see Megan.'

'All part of the job,' Alistair said lightly as they shook hands. He escorted them out of the office then left, no doubt eager to return home to his bed.

Vincenzo sighed as he watched him striding along the corridor. Lowri desperately needed to get some sleep as well but he knew it was pointless suggesting that she go home. All he could do was to try to help any way he could, starting with a plan to avoid anything like this happening again. Megan needed to be in a germ-free environment and that was something he could arrange.

He followed Lowri into the side room where Megan was sleeping, wondering how to convince her that the best place for Megan right now was the villa. There would be far less chance of the child contracting another infection there. Leaving her with her sister while Lowri went to work was merely risking her health unnecessarily, in his view, and he was determined that he was going to make Lowri see sense. Megan's weakened immune system would have a chance to recover at the villa and she would be in a much stronger position when the stem-cell transplant took place.

His heart lurched. Before they could even start to make plans for the transplant, they would have to create this baby.

By five o'clock the following morning, Lowri's head was pounding. The combination of tiredness and stress had brought on a headache and she felt sick from the pain. She closed her eyes, willing the throbbing to abate. She didn't have the time to be ill. Megan needed her and she needed to be here for her too.

'Are you all right?'

Vincenzo's voice sliced through the throbbing in her skull and she winced. Keeping her eyes tightly shut, she nodded. Surprisingly, he had insisted on staying and she had to admit that she had been glad of his company. Having him here had made her feel less scared, if she was honest.

'Yes. I've just got a bit of a headache, that's all.'

'Maybe this will help.'

There was the scrape of chair legs as he stood up. Lowri opened her eyes a crack but the light made her head hurt all the more and she hurriedly closed them again. She heard the measured tread of his footsteps as he came around the bed and she tensed. With her eyes closed she had to rely on her other senses and all of a sudden they seemed to be working overtime.

She bit her lip when she felt his breath stir her hair. He was standing right behind her now, so close that she could feel the heat of his body all down the length of her back, and shivered even though she didn't feel the least bit cold. When his fingers began to stroke her neck, she had to bite back a gasp.

'Wh-what are you doing?' she demanded shakily.

'Massaging your neck. It's what I used to do for Nonna—my grandmother. She suffered from migraines and I found that it helped if I massaged her head and neck.'

'Oh.'

Lowri wasn't sure what to do. Whilst part of her knew she should tell him to stop, she couldn't deny that the gentle pressure of his fingers was having a beneficial effect. In the end she did nothing. She simply sat there while he massaged the tension out of the knotted muscles in her neck. When his hands moved to her head, she didn't protest either. It felt so good to feel his strong fingers moving over her skull. Although he applied only the lightest pressure, she could feel his fingertips burrowing through her hair, warm and firm as he worked his way across her head from back to front.

Lowri sighed when she felt his fingertips start to stroke her brow. Maybe his only intention was to

relieve her headache but she had to admit that she
couldn't recall ever feeling anything as sensual as this
gentle massage. When his thumbs found the throbbing spots at her temples and began to caress them
in a steady circular motion, she groaned.

'Are you all right?' His hands stilled as he bent
forward to look at her.

'Fine.' She dredged up a smile, praying that he
couldn't tell how she really felt. Maybe it was the fact
that her senses were unusually heightened, but she
could feel ripples of awareness running through her.
Her mind flew back to what had happened the previous evening and she realised with a rush of alarm that
if Megan hadn't interrupted them they would have
made love. She had been willing to do so then and
she would be willing to do so now too.

Lowri's eyes flew open. She was so shocked by the
thought that it was a moment before she realised that
her head was no longer aching. Vincenzo's massage
had been highly effective even if it had given rise to
thoughts that she knew would plague her in the days
to come. She wanted to make love with Vincenzo and
not just because she wanted to help Megan either.

'How do you feel now? Is your headache any better?'

The deep rumble of his voice strummed along her
raw nerves and she flinched. It was an effort not to
betray how on edge she felt as she replied. 'Much better. It's more or less gone, in fact.'

She gave a tinkly little laugh and hurried on, not
wanting him to grow suspicious. Vincenzo had agreed
to her demand for another child purely because he
wanted to help Megan. However, if he realised that

her reasons for them making love had taken on a far wider objective, he might refuse to go ahead. Maybe she didn't know him all that well but one thing was certain: he would run a mile if he thought she was trying to trap him into making a commitment.

'You obviously have healing hands, Dr Lombardi,' she said lightly, struggling to get a grip. She couldn't afford to do anything that might make him reconsider his decision to help Megan. 'Your patients must be delighted to be under your care.'

'Offering my patients a massage isn't something I normally do.' He gave a deep laugh, so soft and sensual that Lowri felt her skin prickle with awareness. 'I prefer to reserve my skills as a masseur for the people I care about.'

Oh, it was tempting! So very tempting to ask him if she was one of those people. Lowri just managed to hold back the words but the question glowed, neon bright, inside her head: did Vincenzo care about her?

It was a relief when the door opened as the nurse came in to check Megan's obs. Lowri stood up as Vincenzo moved away and went to the window. It was raining outside, a heavy grey drizzle that blotted out the sky and made everywhere look so dark and dismal that she shivered. Although it was almost June they had seen little sign of summer yet.

All of a sudden she found herself wishing that she could take Megan away for a holiday. Megan would benefit from spending time in the sun but it was unlikely to happen. Even leaving aside the not inconsiderable matter of how much it would cost, she couldn't take any more time off work, although if Megan *did*

need to stay in hospital for any length of time, she
would have to do so.

She sighed as she thought about the problems it
was going to cause. She had used up all her holiday
entitlement as well as a period of compassionate leave
so she would have to ask for unpaid leave of absence.
The thought of how hard it was going to be to pay all
the bills without any money coming in was yet another problem she would have to deal with.

'You're looking very thoughtful.'

Lowri glanced round when Vincenzo came to join
her. The long night had taken its toll on him too, she
realised as she took stock of the shadows under his
eyes and the darkness of stubble on his jaw. He could
have left any time he'd wished and yet he had stayed
with her throughout the night, and all of a sudden she
wanted to know why.

'Why did you stay, Vincenzo? You didn't need to,
so what made you decide to give up a night's sleep?'

'I thought it might help if I was here.'

The lack of emotion in his voice might have put
her off but Lowri sensed that it was deliberate. He
didn't want to admit that he cared what happened to
Megan. The thought warmed her, helped to lift the
black cloud of despondency that had descended on
her, and she smiled at him.

'Thank you. I appreciate it.'

'*Prego!*'

He dismissed her thanks but Lowri knew that he
was pleased all the same. She turned back to the window, watching as the city skyline slowly appeared
through the gloom. It was almost six and she would
have to go and telephone the hospital to warn them she

wouldn't be able to work that day. She frowned, hating the thought of letting down her colleagues once again.

'Tell me, Lowri. Something is troubling you, *sí*? Tell me what it is and maybe we can work out a solution to the problem.'

Maybe it was the new feeling of harmony that seemed to exist between them but she found herself blurting it all out. 'I'm going to have to phone work and tell them I won't be in. I hate letting them down but there's nothing I can do about it. Megan needs me here.'

'Of course. I'm sure they will understand.'

'Oh, I'm sure they will too. That's not the real problem, though. I've already used up all my holiday entitlement plus a fairly lengthy period of compassionate leave.' She grimaced. 'It means that I'll have to apply for unpaid leave of absence if Megan is kept in for very long.'

'And that will cause you some financial difficulties, I imagine.'

Lowri heard the grating note in his voice and immediately wished she hadn't told him that. The last thing she wanted was him thinking that she was asking him for money.

'I'll manage,' she said hurriedly, turning away from the window. The nurse had finished now so she went back to the bed, praying that Vincenzo would let the matter drop. She didn't want his money; it was the last thing she wanted!

'I would be happy to help in any way I can.' He came over to the bed, standing at the opposite side so that she was forced to look at him. Lowri adopted a deliberately neutral expression, hoping he couldn't tell how mortified she felt.

'Thank you but it won't be necessary.' She shrugged. 'I have some savings and I shall manage.'

'I'm sure you will. It appears to me that you are extremely good at managing your affairs, Lowri. However, why should you have to struggle when I can help you?'

'Because I don't want your money, Vincenzo! This has never been about money.'

'I know that.' His eyes met hers, held them fast so that she couldn't look away. 'Your only concern all along has been our daughter and I admire you for that. But please don't cut me out. I want to help and not just because it would make me feel less guilty to be able to do something for Megan. What happens to her truly matters to me, in here.'

He laid his hand over his heart and she felt tears prick her eyes. There wasn't a doubt in her mind that he was telling her the truth and she was deeply moved by his honesty. How could she refuse and deny him the chance to do something for their daughter when it was so important to him?

'I promise that I won't try to cut you out, Vincenzo,' she said softly. 'If you want to help then of course you can.'

'In that case, maybe you will consider an idea I've had.'

'What idea?' she said cautiously.

'Dr Simpson stressed how important it is that Megan should avoid coming into contact with anyone who might be harbouring some kind of infection at the present time, didn't he?'

Lowri nodded, wondering where this was leading. 'That's right.'

'*Bene*. Well, it seems to me that the ideal place for her right now would be the villa.'

'The villa,' she repeated uncertainly.

'*Sì*. My villa at Garda. The place you visited when you came to see me.' He paused to give her time to absorb the idea before continuing. 'My suggestion is that you take Megan there to recuperate. Not only will she be able enjoy the fresh mountain air and the sunshine, but she will be in a relatively germ-free environment.'

'It's kind of you to suggest it,' she began, but he cut her off.

'It's not kind—it makes sense.' His tone held an arrogance that immediately made her bridle.

'Maybe it makes sense to you but I have already explained that I don't want to take any more leave unless it's absolutely necessary,' she retorted.

'And you don't consider it necessary now? Not even after Megan has been rushed back into hospital suffering from some sort of infection?' He stared coldly back at her. 'It seems to me that you need to decide where your priorities lie.'

'That is totally unfair!'

'Is it?' He shrugged. 'I disagree. It sounds to me as though your job is more important to you than she is.'

'Nothing is more important to me than Megan!' she said, deeply hurt by the accusation. 'However, we don't all have the luxury of family money to fall back on. If I don't work, we shall probably lose our home. Is that what you want, Vincenzo, that our daughter should be left homeless?'

'Of course not!' He sounded rattled by the suggestion and Lowri couldn't stop the small thrill of pleasure that ran through her for having pierced his armour.

'Then you must understand why I can't accept your offer?'

'No, I don't understand. I don't understand why you are willing to put Megan's health at risk when there is no need.' His tone was icy and yet beneath its chill she sensed a passion that filled her with heat. All of a sudden she knew that this was important to him even though she wasn't sure why.

'You and Megan can stay at the villa for as long as you like. I shall pay all your bills here and meet all your expenses while you are there.' He looked her squarely in the eyes and she shivered when she saw the determination on his face. Vincenzo intended to get his own way about this no matter what she said or did and it was more than a little scary to realise it.

'It will solve two major problems. Not only will Megan be able to recuperate and regain her strength but it will give us the opportunity we need to put our plan into action. If that doesn't make sense to you, Lowri, then I don't know what does!'

CHAPTER EIGHT

Vincenzo stood on the terrace and watched as the sun set over Lake Garda. It was a sight that never failed to captivate him yet he found his attention wandering that night. Had he done the right thing by virtually *forcing* Lowri to bring Megan here or had he merely made a difficult situation more complicated?

He had never stopped to consider what he might be getting into when he had made the suggestion; he had seen it simply as the solution to their problems. However, now he found himself wondering about how it was going to affect him. How could he maintain his distance, as he needed to do, when Lowri was living under his roof?

'She's asleep at last. She was so excited when she saw her bedroom and all the toys you've bought for her that I didn't think I'd ever persuade her to settle down. You really shouldn't spoil her like that, Vincenzo.'

Vincenzo glanced round when Lowri came to join him. She was still wearing the clothes she had worn to travel in, lightweight cotton jeans and a pale blue shirt, and he found himself thinking how pretty she looked. Most of the women he knew dressed far more formally, choosing clothes that made a statement about their position in life. However, Lowri didn't appear to be concerned about how other people viewed her and he found her attitude refreshing.

'She's had a tough time in the past two weeks. Having to go back into hospital was a real blow for her and she deserves a treat,' he said, reining in his thoughts. That he was attracted to Lowri wasn't in question but he must never forget that it was Megan who mattered. Maybe they had grown closer as they had sat at Megan's bedside while she had fought off the infection, but the truth was that Lowri would never have contacted him in the first place if it weren't for their daughter.

The thought was strangely depressing. Vincenzo swung round, refusing to dwell on it. 'How about a drink? You've had a busy day and a glass of wine might help you unwind.'

'I really should unpack,' she began, and then shrugged. 'Why not? I can unpack later, can't I?'

'Of course.'

Vincenzo went inside and took a bottle of Pinot Grigio out of the wine cooler. Maria, his housekeeper, had prepared a tray of nibbles before she had left and he took that outside as well. Lowri was still standing where he had left her and he paused, studying the line of her back, the tilt of her head, simply soaking up the sheer familiarity of her. She had been back in his life for a matter of weeks and yet it felt as though she had been an important part of his world for ever.

The thought alarmed him. Vincenzo could feel his heart pounding as he set the tray on the table. He uncorked the wine, aware that his hands weren't as steady as they should have been. He was getting in way too deep and he needed to take several steps back. Although it was understandable if the past two weeks had brought him and Lowri closer, he couldn't afford to let that influence him. So maybe he *did* want to help Megan, and maybe he *was* willing to have another child with Lowri if it meant they could achieve that objective, but was he really prepared to make a lifetime's commitment to her?

He had sworn he would never marry again after his divorce. Even though he and Carla had entered into the marriage with their eyes open, it hadn't worked. He had wanted a wife who would support his career and not make too many demands on him, and Carla had wanted the security that a wedding ring would afford her.

As a top-flight commercial lawyer, she had grown tired of being hit on by her clients and had found it useful to have a wealthy husband in the background.

It had worked very well too until Carla had decided that she had wanted more from life. She had wanted a family and that had been something he had always ruled out. Their divorce had been inevitable after that, but had he really changed so much that he was ready to consider the idea? Could he see himself not only in the role of father to Megan and to this new baby they might have but as Lowri's husband?

Vincenzo's hands shook even more as he poured the wine. Whilst he was still determined to do whatever was necessary to help Megan, he knew that he needed to reassess the situation. He came to a swift decision, aware that he would be unable to think things through with the necessary clarity if he was around Lowri. Lowri made him *feel* all sorts of things; however, she didn't make it easy for him to think!

'I shall be returning to Milan in the morning.' He handed her a glass and sat down. He took a sip of the wine, hoping it would steady him. He needed to be strong, needed to deal with this situation on his own and in his own way too.

'Oh. I didn't realise you were going back to Milan so soon,' she began, then shrugged. 'Of course. You must have things to attend to.'

'I need to settle on a date for when I return to work,' Vincenzo said as smoothly as he could. He took another swallow of the wine, calling himself all sorts of unflattering names when he realised that he was disappointed that she hadn't tried to persuade him to stay. If truth be told, she must be as eager for some time on her own as he was.

'Ah. Well, that's good, isn't it? You must feel that your arm has healed if you're planning to return to Theatre.' She smiled brightly as she raised her glass. 'Here's to a successful return, Vincenzo. I'm sure your colleagues will be delighted to have you back.'

'*Grazie.*' He responded to her toast, wondering wryly if his return would be greeted with very much enthusiasm. From what he had heard that day, his team seemed to have been coping extremely well without him.

He pushed the thought aside, not wanting anything to deter him. Returning to work would give him the breathing space he needed to decide how to handle this situation. He had a choice: he could maintain his distance and simply make financial provision for Megan and the new baby, or he could become a proper father to them with *all* that it entailed—assuming that Lowri would agree, of course.

He sighed. It appeared that the decision wasn't wholly his after all. It very much depended on what Lowri wanted.

It was shortly after ten when Lowri excused herself and went up to her room. It had been a pleasant evening and Vincenzo had gone out of his way put her at ease. She had grown increasingly nervous as the time had approached for her and Megan to travel to the villa, but if Vincenzo continued to behave as he had done today then it appeared that she had nothing to fear.

She certainly couldn't fault the arrangements he had made to get them there. He had taken heed of Dr Simpson's advice to keep Megan away from anyone who might be harbouring an infection by hiring a private plane to fly them to Milan, where they'd been met by a chauffeur-driven limousine.

In a remarkably short space of time they had arrived at the villa, where his housekeeper, Maria, had been waiting to greet them. It had been a world away from the journey she had made a few weeks earlier and she couldn't help comparing the two. It was obvious that Vincenzo had both the money and the means to make things happen. She wasn't sure why it made her feel slightly uneasy to know that.

She pushed the thought aside as she opened her suitcase and took out a pair of pyjamas. Opening the connecting door to Megan's room, she checked that the little girl was fast asleep before going to take a shower, frowning as she looked around. The white-

painted bed with its golden coronet above supporting
a drift of pale pink net was every little girl's dream.
The rest of the furniture was white too, the ward-
robes and chests exquisitely painted with fairies and
tiny woodland creatures. There was even a toy chest
under the window stuffed full of dolls and soft toys,
plus a shelf of brand-new books.

Whether Vincenzo had chosen everything himself
or had asked his housekeeper to do it, she wasn't sure.
However, the fact that he had gone to so much trouble
and expense to prepare the room surprised her. Surely,
it was a waste of time and money if he didn't intend
to play a permanent role in Megan's life?

The thought stayed with her while she showered
and got ready for bed. Switching off the bedside lamp,
she lay in the darkness and tried to work it all out but
she was too tired to make sense of it. She had no real
idea what Vincenzo was planning and would have to
wait and see what happened. Maybe he would stay in
contact with her and Megan and maybe he wouldn't,
and it was unsettling not to know what the future
held in store. After all, his decision would affect them
all—her, Megan and this new baby they were planning to have.

She rolled over, burying her hot face in the pillow.
By tacit consent they hadn't discussed their plans for
the baby in the last few weeks. Megan had been so
ill and they had concentrated on helping her to get
better. However, they would need to finalise the arrangements soon and the thought made her feel all
jittery inside.

Although she was aware that she and Vincenzo
had grown closer during the long hours they had sat

at Megan's bedside, she still didn't feel that she knew him all that well. He was such a contradiction, one minute cool and distant and the next warm and sympathetic. It was little wonder that it was so hard to get the measure of him. However, before they embarked on making this baby, she needed to be sure about what they were doing. Although she desperately wanted to help Megan, having another child wasn't something to be undertaken lightly. For *any* reason.

Lowri took a deep breath as she finally acknowledged the truth. She wanted this baby for its own sake and not just because it could save its sister's life. She knew that she would love it with all her heart, no matter what happened. However, before she went ahead, she needed to be sure that Vincenzo wanted it too. For the child's sake, it was important that she was sure he wouldn't regret it.

The sun was streaming through the windows when Lowri awoke the following morning. Reaching for the clock, she was shocked to discover that it was gone nine a.m. Scrambling out of bed, she ran to the adjoining room but there was no sign of Megan. She hurried downstairs, her heart pounding as she wondered where Megan had gone. The little girl didn't know her way around the villa yet and the thought that she might have wandered outside filled Lowri with dread. Anything could have happened to her!

'*Buon giorno*, Lowri. Come and join us. We were just about to have breakfast, weren't we, *tesoro*?'

Lowri spun round, feeling relief overwhelm her when she saw Megan standing on the terrace, holding Vincenzo's hand. Hurrying over to them, she swept her daughter up into her arms and kissed her. 'You gave me such a fright! I didn't know where you'd gone when I found your room was empty.'

'Megan was thirsty so she came downstairs to get a drink,' Vincenzo explained. He ran his hand over the child's head, his fingers gently brushing her skull. 'She helped me prepare breakfast, didn't you, *amore*? She cut up all the fruit, in fact.'

'I don't let her use a knife,' Lowri said quickly, then flushed. It sounded so petty to remonstrate with him when he had taken care of Megan while she'd been asleep.

'No?' He shrugged. 'Well, she made a very good job of it. The fruit looks delicious, doesn't it?'

He swept a hand towards the table and Lowri had to hide her smile when she saw the heap of fruit piled into the dish. Some of the peaches looked decidedly battered and the strawberries had a distinctly squashed air about them. Looking up, she laughed when she met Vincenzo's eyes and saw the amusement they held.

'It does indeed. Very tempting.'

'Bene.' He led Megan to the table and sat her down then pulled out a chair for Lowri. His fingers brushed the back of her neck as he got her settled. 'I'll leave you to make a start while I fetch the coffee. Maria doesn't arrive until later so I'm afraid we have to fend for ourselves at breakfast.'

'That's fine,' Lowri said swiftly, trying to contain the shiver that passed through her when she felt the warmth of his fingers seeping through the thin cotton of her pyjama top. She took a deep breath as she helped Megan spoon some fruit into her bowl. She had to stop this, had to stop being so *aware* of him all the time. At the end of the day she must never forget that Vincenzo wasn't interested in her. He was only interested in helping Megan.

Vincenzo picked up the coffee pot then took a deep breath. He had to stop this, had to stop reacting every time he was near Lowri. He had touched her purely by accident yet he could feel tingles of awareness spreading through his entire body and silently cursed himself.

He had never responded this way to a woman before and it would be foolish to allow himself to do so now. He needed to decide what he intended to do without anything distracting him. His feelings for Lowri weren't the issue. It was the effect it could have on his life if he made a commitment to her and the children that mattered. His whole existence would be affected, all the plans he had made would need to be changed. Quite frankly, he wasn't sure if he could cope with such a major upheaval.

He took the coffee pot outside and put it on the table, doing his best to present a calm front. Normally, he had no difficulty doing so—his natural demeanour was cool and aloof. However, it was hard to be distant or aloof as Megan chattered away, excitedly pointing out all the things that captured her attention, like a bright red butterfly that landed on some flowers and the vapour trail a plane had left in the sky.

'I haven't seen her so animated for ages,' Lowri said quietly, as the little girl jumped up to chase the butterfly. 'Being here is already doing her the power of good.'

'She needed a change of scene,' Vincenzo replied

smoothly, although his heart lifted at the thought that his plan had been so successful. It helped lessen the guilt he felt about the way he had…well, *bullied* Lowri into agreeing to come here. Even though he knew it had been for her own good, he still wished that he hadn't needed to take such a hard line.

'She did. She's been through so much and having to go back into hospital while they sorted out that infection was the last straw.' She shook her head. 'I've never seen her looking so down as she's done these past few weeks.'

'It's been hard for her. And hard for you, too.' He sighed, knowing that he had to say it even though it worried him to be so open about his feelings. 'I only had a taste of what you've been through, Lowri, and I know how difficult I found it.'

'Did you?' she said in surprise, and he grimaced.

'*Sì*. Seeing how ill Megan was wasn't easy.'

'I didn't realise that,' she said slowly, looking at him with wide hazel eyes. 'You always seemed so… well, so *together* when we were at the hospital.'

'Did I?' He gave a small shrug, not sure if it was a relief to know that he had managed to fool her. Whilst he preferred to keep his emotions under wraps, he would hate it if she thought he didn't care.

'Yes. I found it really hard, if I'm honest. I don't know why but seeing her so ill again really got to me this time.' Her voice caught. 'I don't think I'd have coped half as well if you hadn't been there, Vincenzo.'

It was his turn to look surprised. 'Really?'

'Uh-huh.' She gave a slightly sheepish laugh. 'A couple of times I nearly lost it but you were there, looking so calm and so sure that everything was going to be all right. It helped tremendously.'

'I had no idea.' He broke off and shook his head. 'All I can say is that I never suspected you were so worried.'

'Good. If you didn't realise it then Megan didn't either.' She gave him a quick smile as she reached for the coffee pot. 'I must be a better actress than I thought.'

Vincenzo smiled politely but the comment had touched a nerve. He had assumed that he had got to know Lowri rather well in the past few weeks but now he could see that he had been mistaken. Although he might know her on the surface, he didn't really know what made her tick, did he?

It was worrying to realise that he had made assumptions that weren't based on anything solid. If he was to work out what he intended to do, he needed to base any decisions he made on facts. He had never been comfortable dealing with emotions. Emotions skewed his judgement, made it impossible for him to be sure about what he was doing. If he allowed his emotions to influence him then he could end up making a terrible mistake.

Vincenzo decided that he needed to leave immediately. As soon as he had finished eating, he excused himself and went to fetch his briefcase. Lowri was standing in the hall when he came out of his study and he paused, struggling to control the leap his heart gave when he saw her. She was still wearing her pyjamas, pale pink cotton sprigged with tiny rosebuds.

There was nothing overtly seductive about the outfit yet he could feel the blood running hotly through his veins. It was an effort to smile coolly when what he really wanted to do was take her in his arms and kiss her until they were both senseless.

'Maria will be in before noon. She will prepare lunch for you and dinner as well. If there's anything you need, she can get it for you too.'

'Thank you. You've thought of everything, Vincenzo. I know I wasn't exactly keen to come here when you first suggested it, but I'm sure it's going to give Megan the boost she needs.'

'I'm glad.' He gave a small shrug. 'I still feel a little guilty about the way I bullied you into falling in with my plans.'

'Then don't. There's no need, really.' She gave him a quick smile. 'So when are you planning on coming back?'

'I'm not sure,' he hedged, trying not to get carried away by the thought that she might miss him. Of course she wouldn't miss him, not when she had Megan to think about. His tone was flat when he continued but it was better than letting her guess how disappointed he felt. 'It will take me a few days to catch up with what's been happening in my absence, I imagine.'

'Of course,' she said quietly, and he hated to hear how reserved she sounded and know that it was all his fault. 'Do you have a phone number where I can reach you?'

'Yes, of course.' He took out his wallet and handed her a card listing his contact number at the hospital. 'You can get me on this. If I'm not available then leave a message with my secretary and I'll call you back.'

'Thank you.' Her tone was dry; it made him wish

that he had given her his mobile number but it was too late to backtrack. She smiled coolly. 'Don't worry, I'll be discreet. I'm sure you don't want people knowing what we're planning on doing.'

'It would be best if we keep the details to ourselves,' he agreed, trying not to let her see that her reaction had stung. He returned his wallet to his pocket, wondering why he was so sensitive all of a sudden. Normally he paid no heed to what people thought of him but he seemed unusually susceptible when it came to Lowri. He didn't want her thinking badly of him, strangely enough.

He cleared his throat, uncomfortable with that thought too. 'I shall call you tonight to check that you are all right.'

'There's no need. I'm sure we'll be fine.'

The chill in her voice brought the colour to his cheeks and he turned away, not wanting her to witness his discomfort. 'As you wish. *Ciao!*'

He strode out of the door, pausing when he heard Megan calling him. Turning, he smiled when he saw her hurtling across the hall. Dropping his briefcase onto the floor, he swung her up into his arms. 'You must slow down, *tesoro*. You could slip and hurt yourself. *Sì?*'

'*Sì.*' Megan wrapped her arms around his neck. She stared at him with eyes that were identical to the ones he saw in the mirror each morning when he was shaving. 'Where are you going, Vincenzo? I want to come with you.'

'I would love you to come, *amore*, but it's a long way and you would get very bored.' He buzzed her cheek with his lips, feeling tenderness overwhelm him when her small arms tightened around his neck. His tone was gruffer than normal but it was the first time he had experienced the sheer depth of love that a father felt for his child so he could be excused for being rather emotional. 'You stay here with Mummy and I shall come back to see you very soon.'

'Promise?' Megan demanded.

'Promise.'

He put her down, his heart catching all over again when he looked up and saw the expression on Lowri's face. That she had been moved by what she had witnessed was obvious. Without stopping to think, he went to her and dropped a kiss on her cheek, his lips lingering for the merest fraction of a second. If he allowed himself more than this token kiss he would never leave her, never be able to assess this situation, think it all through clearly and rationally.

He drew back, staring into her eyes before he turned away. Megan shouted goodbye and he responded but Lowri didn't say a word. Vincenzo got into his car and gunned the engine then drove out of the gates. The road leading into Garda was as busy as ever, tourists and locals vying for space, but he felt none of his usual impatience. He wasn't in a rush to get to Milan, as he normally was. Up till now work had been his *raison d'être* but not any more. His priorities had changed now that he was a father.

He gripped the steering-wheel as panic assailed him. It was going to be harder than he had thought to make the right decision. It wasn't just he who would be affected but Megan too and he didn't want to disappoint her, to let her down.

He didn't want to let Lowri down either but how

could he guarantee that it wouldn't happen? How could he be sure that at some point in the future she wouldn't regret contacting him?

His heart ached as he followed the signs for Milan. He knew so little about what it took to be a good father. Even if he tried his best, he could still fail. The thought of Lowri's disappointment if he turned out like his own father was very hard to bear. It might be better if he called a halt rather than risk that happening. Oh, he had agreed to give her another baby and he would keep his promise, but after that it would be better for everyone if he faded into the background. He would make financial provision for Megan and the baby but he wouldn't have any further contact with them. He would do his duty and that was all.

Vincenzo took a deep breath and used it to shore up the pain that flooded through him. Once this baby was born that would be it. He and Lowri would get on with their lives. Separately.

CHAPTER NINE

A WEEK PASSED and Lowri didn't hear a word from Vincenzo apart from a brief phone call the first night. She tried to tell herself that he was busy and didn't have the time to call, but it was hard to believe that. Surely he could spare a couple of minutes to check on Megan?

As the days passed, she found herself growing increasingly angry about the way he had seemingly abandoned them, especially when Megan kept asking when he was coming back. However, it wasn't until the Friday morning that she decided to take matters into her own hands.

She had been monitoring her monthly cycle and she knew that in a few days it would be the optimum time for her to conceive. Although she wasn't in a rush to sleep with Vincenzo, on a practical level the sooner they got it over and done with the better. She called the number he had given her and left a message with his secretary, asking him to phone her back. Megan was playing in the swimming pool, watched over by a doting Maria, so once she had made the call, Lowri went to relieve her.

Maria had proved to be a godsend, looking after

Megan while Lowri went for a walk or visited the local shops. Her husband, Alfredo, was the gardener and he too had endless patience as Megan followed him around, asking questions. Although Alfredo spoke very little English, somehow he and Megan managed to communicate. Lowri knew that being at the villa was doing Megan a world of good but she still couldn't shrug off her anger at Vincenzo's behaviour. It seemed doubly unacceptable after what had happened the morning he had left for Milan.

She dismissed the thought, knowing it was pointless reading anything into what had gone on. Maybe Vincenzo had appeared to be deeply moved by Megan's reaction to him leaving but if he had cared that much, he would have phoned to see how she was. Her mouth thinned as she made her way to the pool. Vincenzo didn't really care about Megan. And he certainly didn't care about her!

She spent an hour playing in the pool with Megan. As soon as the little girl started to tire, she lifted her out and took her inside. There was still an hour to go before lunch and Megan would benefit from a nap beforehand. Although Megan's health was definitely improving, she tired easily and Lowri took care to make sure that she rested during the day.

She stripped off Megan's swimsuit and popped on a nightie then persuaded her to lie down on the bed with one of her new dolls. She soon fell asleep so Lowri went to her own room, meaning to read until Megan woke up. She had just opened her book when the phone in the hall rang and the next moment she heard Maria calling her.

She ran down the stairs, her heart racing as she

wondered if Vincenzo had finally deigned to phone her. Picking up the receiver, she held it to her ear. 'Yes?'

'It's Vincenzo. My secretary told me that you had telephoned. There is nothing wrong, I hope?'

He sounded concerned but Lowri had no intention of being mollified. 'And what if there was something wrong? What would you do, Vincenzo? Come haring back here like a knight in shining armour to sort it all out?' She laughed scornfully. 'I doubt it. Not when you haven't even bothered to phone!'

There was a brief silence before he replied. 'I am sorry. It was remiss of me not to phone before now. I can only apologise.'

'Apologies cost nothing, though, do they? It's actions that speak loudest of all.'

'Meaning what precisely?' There was the faintest rumble of anger in his voice, just the tiniest ruffle marring its silky-smooth surface. Lowri felt a thrill of pleasure run through her when she realised that she had managed to arouse a reaction.

'*Meaning* that if you'd cared anything at all about Megan then you would have phoned to find out how she was. It's ironic, really. I'm the one who claimed to be a better actress than I thought I was, but you're the one who actually deserves all the plaudits. Your performance the morning you left for Milan deserved an Oscar!'

Stony silence greeted her comment. Lowri held her breath, determined that she wasn't going to break it. As far as she was concerned, it was Vincenzo who was at fault, not her.

'I take it that you phoned for a reason and not simply because you felt the need to berate me for my failings?'

His voice was so cold that she shivered. Lowri could feel chills running down her spine but that, undoubtedly, had been his intention. Vincenzo was the master of the cold put-down, the Bard when it came to choosing words that would have the most effect on anyone who crossed him. However, she refused to become another of his hapless victims.

'Well, I certainly didn't phone so we could have a pleasant little chat.' She laughed coolly. 'That would have been a complete waste of both our time.'

'Indeed. So what is it that you need to tell me, Lowri?'

His tone was still on the chilly side but there was a hint of amusement in it that surprised her. Warmed her. Wormed its way through her anger. It was hard not to show how disconcerted she felt, only she wouldn't give him the satisfaction of knowing that he had thrown her off balance.

'I thought you should know that I shall reach the most fertile point in my monthly cycle in a few days' time. If we hope to conceive this baby then we shall have to do something about it.'

Vincenzo gripped hold of the desk as the room started to spin. Do something about it or, in other words, sleep together!

'Are you still there?'

'*Sì.*' He cleared his throat but he could feel his heart racing almost out of control. It was an effort to appear calm when it was the last thing he felt. 'Thank you for letting me know. You were right to do so. We cannot afford to waste any time if we are to help Megan.'

'Precisely.'

Lowri's tone sounded calm enough but he caught nuance of some other emotion just beneath the surface and his heart raced all the harder. The thought of sleeping with him had aroused a lot of emotions inside her too, although it would be foolish to imagine that she felt the same as he did.

The thought was like a douse of cold water. Vincenzo felt his euphoria disappear, swept away by the reality of the situation. When he and Lowri slept together, they wouldn't be making love but a baby. And that was the only reason why she was prepared to go through with it.

'I shall make arrangements to return to the villa,' he said in his most businesslike tone.

'So you still want to go ahead? You haven't changed your mind? I thought maybe you had when you didn't phone.'

'No, I haven't changed my mind. Have you?'

'I…uhm…no. Not really.'

'But you do have doubts?' he persisted, sensing she was holding something back.

'Not doubts. More concerns, if anything.'

It was like getting blood from a stone, getting her to answer. Vincenzo realised that they needed to discuss this; however, before he could question her further there was a knock on the door and Fabio Russo, one of his junior registrars, poked his head into the room.

'Yes? What is it?' Vincenzo snapped, making no effort whatsoever to disguise his annoyance at the interruption.

'Mi scusi,' the young man muttered, looking scared out of his wits. 'Pronto Soccorso has phoned. They have a child with a serious head trauma and need you to see him.'

'Tell them I shall be there shortly,' Vincenzo instructed curtly, then immediately wished he hadn't been so abrupt when the younger man scurried away.

'I can tell that you're busy, Vincenzo, so I won't keep you. Goodbye.'

She hung up before he could reply. Vincenzo stared at the receiver for a moment then slammed it down onto the rest and put his head in his hands. He needed to resolve whatever issues Lowri had but he couldn't do that until he had attended to his patient. He had never felt so torn before, never allowed anything to take precedence over his work, but this was different. This concerned Lowri and Megan and this new baby they might or might not have.

His heart contracted in sudden fear. If Lowri had changed her mind, then what would it mean for Megan? What chance would she have without this stem-cell transplant? He had been tested as a potential donor while they had been at the hospital, but he hadn't been a good enough match either so they appeared to have run out of options. Oh, maybe there was a chance that a donor would be found at some point but would it be soon enough? Would Megan live long enough to receive the treatment she needed so desperately?

His head hurt as he made his way to Pronto Soccorso. There was so much to think about, so many emotionally charged issues to deal with, and he was a novice at it. All he could do was his best and if that meant persuading Lowri to have this baby, that's what he intended to do.

Heat roared along his veins as he followed the attending physician into Resus. His reasons for wanting to make love with Lowri might be of the very highest order primarily, but he couldn't deny that there were other, far less lofty reasons for doing so too!

Lowri felt on edge all afternoon long. The conversation she'd had with Vincenzo had done more harm than good. She regretted being so waspish with him, even though she felt that she had been right to take him to task.

He *should have* phoned to check on Megan, yet she had a feeling that it hadn't been a lack of interest that had stopped him. His failure to get in touch had been deliberate, thought out, rationalised. And it was why he had felt the need to distance himself that worried her most. Whilst she had some qualms about them having this baby, she was still prepared to go ahead. Was Vincenzo still willing to go through with it though, despite what he had said? That was the big question.

The thought stayed with her even though she tried to push it to one side. The nap had done Megan good so once lunch was over Lowri took her for a walk to the nearest village. There was just a handful of shops there but Megan enjoyed looking at the brightly painted pottery and other knick-knacks made for the tourist trade. There was a coach parked near the tiny walled harbour, which was the town's main attraction, so Lowri steered clear of there. Although it was doubtful if Megan would catch anything from the tourists, there was no point taking chances. She led her up a side street instead and bought her a miniature tea set from one of the shops and took her home. It had been a pleasant interlude, even if it hadn't managed to dispel all the thoughts whizzing around her head. She would need to talk to Vincenzo to do that, always assuming that he would talk to her.

She helped Megan arrange her new tea service on the terrace, filling the tiny pot with orange juice and begging some miniature cookies from Maria. While Megan ran upstairs to fetch her dolls, Lowri took the opportunity to pour herself a drink. She carried it outside and stopped dead when she found Vincenzo standing on the terrace, staring in bemusement at the tiny plates and cups. He looked up when he heard her approaching and shook his head.

'I was beginning to think that I had wandered into a different dimension. This isn't Lilliput, is it?'

'No. Or at least it wasn't when I last checked.' Lowri chuckled, feeling some of her anxiety melt away. Nothing too serious could have happened otherwise he wouldn't be able to make jokes like that, would he?

'Thank heavens for that.' He smiled. 'I'm not sure I'd make a very good giant. All that fee-fi-fo-fumming would get me down after a while.'

'Maybe you should choose a different fairy-tale character?' she suggested, putting her glass of lemonade on the table. 'Which was your favourite when you were a child?'

'I don't remember.'

He held his smile but all the warmth seemed to have gone out of it for some reason. Lowri frowned, wondering what she had said to trigger that reaction. However, before she could ask him, Megan came back, squealing with excitement when she saw Vincenzo.

'You've come back! Mummy said you were too busy but I knew you'd come.' She ran over and grabbed hold of his hand. ''Cos you promised, didn't you?'

'*Sì*. And I always try to keep my promises, *tesoro*.'

Bending, he dropped a gentle kiss on the child's cheek. Lowri looked away when she felt her eyes fill with tears. She knew it was silly but she couldn't help it. Megan really seemed to like Vincenzo and he seemed to like her too. They had a genuine rapport and she could only hope that it would continue, although there was no guarantee. Vincenzo hadn't made any promises about the future and she mustn't forget that.

The thought of Megan's disappointment if he disappeared from her life was very hard to swallow. However, Lowri knew that she had to face facts, and the biggest fact of all was Vincenzo's aversion to having a family. The thought set loose all her misgivings once again. Was it right to bring another child into the world when it might not have any contact with its father?

When she had set out to persuade Vincenzo to help her, she had given little thought to what would happen beyond saving Megan's life. Now, however, she could see that she needed to think everything through very carefully. She could imagine the detrimental effect it would have on Megan if she never saw Vincenzo, but how much worse would it be for the baby to grow up believing that he or she had been born for one reason only—to save its sister's life? No child should feel it was second best, and she couldn't bear to think that her child might grow up believing that.

Her spine stiffened. It was something they urgently needed to discuss. She needed to know exactly where she stood before they went any further. The question was simple: did Vincenzo intend to play a role in his children's lives or not?

Vincenzo closed his eyes, savouring the all too rare feeling of peace that filled him. It was just gone eight and Lowri was putting Megan to bed. As a treat, the little girl had been allowed to stay up late and have supper with them, but it had been obvious by the time they'd finished that she had been flagging. Now, as he heard Lowri's footsteps crossing the terrace, he opened his eyes and smiled up at her.

'That was quick. She went out like a light, did she?'

'Yes.' She laughed as she sat down beside him on the cushioned lounger. 'I didn't bother giving her a bath. She could barely keep her eyes open when I was undressing her. Anyway, she spent ages in the pool this morning so she can't be *that* grubby!'

'A little dirt never hurt anyone,' Vincenzo observed lightly, trying to keep his mind on what they were discussing. He sighed under his breath. It was a losing battle when Lowri was sitting so close to him that he could smell the lemon scent of her shampoo and feel the warmth of her skin.

'Did you get that from your mother?' She turned slightly to look at him and smiled. 'It was one of my mother's favourite sayings too, funnily enough.'

'I don't remember but it can't have been my mother. She died when I was very small.'

'Oh, I'm sorry. I had no idea.' Reaching out, she covered his hand with hers. 'How awful for you, Vincenzo. Mum was such an important part of my life. She was a feisty little Welsh woman—which accounts for my and Cerys's names. However, she was the kindest person anyone could hope to meet and we all adored her. I can't imagine how awful it must have been for you, having to grow up without your mother.'

'As I said, I was very young when she died, barely two, in fact.' He shrugged, trying to keep a rein on his emotions. He rarely thought about his mother and how different his life might have been if she had lived but Lowri's response had let loose a lot of very painful thoughts. 'What is that saying about you don't miss what you've never had? I think that explains it.'

'Ye-es.'

She sounded unconvinced but at least she didn't pursue the subject and he was glad. Talking about his childhood wasn't something he planned on doing tonight... Or ever, he swiftly amended. He cleared his throat, determined that he was going to deal with the current crisis in the calmest way possible. That was why he had decided to drive to the villa tonight.

Even though he'd been bone tired after an afternoon in Theatre, he'd known that he needed to sort everything out with Lowri, make sure that she was still prepared to go ahead and have this baby. Megan's whole future depended on it and he needed to convince her that any doubts she might be harbouring were groundless.

If he could.

The thought that he might fail hit him hard but he knew that he had to be strong. After all, it was Lowri who had come up with this plan in the first place and she must have felt that it could work. Obviously, her concerns were recent and it was up to him to convince her that it was still the right thing to do, to gain her trust and, indeed, prove his worth.

It was daunting to think he might fail but Vincenzo gave no sign of unease as he stood up. Picking up the bottle of wine, he topped up their glasses. 'We may as well finish this while we talk.'

'Thank you.' Lowri accepted the glass but instead of drinking any of the wine she put it on the table. 'We need to talk, don't we, Vincenzo?'

'*Sì.* That is why I came back tonight. I could tell from our conversation earlier in the day that you have issues that need to be addressed.'

He resumed his seat, crossing one leg over the other in the hope that he could present a calm front. In truth, he had never felt more keyed up in his life but he refused to show it, refused to worry her even more by letting her see that he was worried too.

He sighed. Why had everything become so damned complicated? Why had he suddenly started trying to second-guess someone else's thoughts and feelings? It was something he had never done before and he was particularly bad at it. Nevertheless, he would have to get himself up to speed if he hoped to persuade her to go ahead with this plan.

The thought sent a shaft of heat through him and he rolled the glass between his palms to cool them. He needed to persuade Lowri to make love with him. He needed to do it so that Megan might have the chance to live a long and happy life. That had been Lowri's aim from the outset. She hadn't contacted him because she had missed him. She hadn't wasted the past five years wishing that they had stayed together. She probably hadn't given him any thought at all, in fact, except initially, when she had found out she was having his child.

His heart ached as he forced himself to face the facts. He was simply someone she'd had a brief affair with. Someone who had come into her life and turned it upside down. He meant nothing to her beyond that and it made him see how difficult it was going to be to convince her that he was sincere about wanting to be there for their children.

In her eyes he was all negatives. There were very few plus points he could lay claim to apart from his wealth and she seemed indifferent to that. So if she did have doubts, how was he going to persuade her that he was worth taking a chance on? That he wouldn't let her down, that he would support her and the children for ever when he wasn't sure he was capable of doing it himself?

Vincenzo closed his eyes and did something he hadn't done for years, not since his grandmother had died. He prayed.

CHAPTER TEN

LOWRI COULD FEEL her heart pounding as the silence lengthened. Vincenzo was sitting there with his eyes closed and she had no idea what he was thinking.

She jumped when his eyes opened and he pinned her with a look that made her feel as though he was searching her very soul. She wanted to ask him what he was thinking, what she could do to help him, but the words wouldn't come. She could only wait and see what happened.

Her breath caught when he suddenly got up. Walking to the end of the terrace, he stared across the lake. The sun had almost disappeared now and the shadows were turning the water to the colour of pewter. The last of the ferry boats had docked but there were still some sailboats out on the water. She watched the glow from their lights while her mind raced. What was Vincenzo going to say? That he had changed his mind about this baby, that he no longer wanted to go ahead, that he didn't need or want the responsibility of another child? The thought was too much.

'Vincenzo...'

'Do you still want to go ahead and have this baby?'

They both spoke and both stopped. Lowri bit her

lip when he turned and she saw the anguish on his face. Although this might be difficult for her, it was no easier for him and that was something she hadn't taken account of. Not once had she considered how hard it must be for him to agree to such a major undertaking.

'Yes. But if you've changed your mind then there's nothing I can do, is there?' she said hollowly.

'I haven't. If anything, I'm more committed to the idea than I ever was.'

His tone was flat yet she could see the gleam of real emotion in his eyes and knew he was merely feigning indifference. Why? Because he was afraid to admit to his feelings? Afraid to acknowledge that he possessed any?

Her heart overflowed with compassion. Maybe he appeared to have everything anyone could wish for—wealth and prestige in both his private and his professional life. But how awful must it be to have to constantly hide his feelings, to pretend that he didn't feel anything?

The thought was so overwhelming that Lowri acted on instinct. Getting up, she went and put her arms around him, like she would have done to Megan if the little girl was afraid. He felt so tense and she drew him closer, hoping that the contact with another human being would help. That was all she wanted to do, to help him, to make this easier for him, and yet the minute she had her arms around him, everything changed. Feeling the solid strength of his body pressed against hers set off a response she had never anticipated.

Lowri sucked in her breath when she felt a shaft of awareness strike her like a bolt of lightning. All of a sudden she was conscious of every noise, each smell, each and every touch. She flinched when she felt his shirt brush against her cheek, held her breath as she inhaled the scent of his skin, tried her best to fill her mind with white noise that would block out the sound of his breathing, but it was hopeless. She seemed to be drowning in sensations, soaking them up like a sponge, absorbing them into her very being; becoming part of him as he was becoming part of her.

'Lowri.'

Her name was the softest whisper yet she shuddered. When she felt his hand lift her chin, she closed her eyes. She was too afraid of what she might see on his face and what he might see on hers to open them.

'Lowri, look at me, *cara*.'

His tone was so gentle that she couldn't resist. Lowri opened her eyes and gazed up at him, knowing that he must see how she was feeling, each doubt, every fear, every little temptation.

He uttered something rough under his breath, not words but something far less structured. Bending, he placed his mouth over hers and kissed her. Lowri just had a moment to draw breath, a mere instant to decide what to do, whether to push him away or respond, and then the moment was lost. How could she push him away when she needed his kiss so badly?

Her arms fastened around his neck while she drew his head down so she could deepen the kiss, her heart pounding when she felt his tongue slide between her lips. There was no hesitation, no fumbling, no attempt to hold back on his part or on hers. If she needed this kiss then he did too!

They were both breathing hard when he raised

his head, both feeling stunned, she suspected, by the speed of their passion, but she didn't regret it and prayed he didn't either. Desire like this shouldn't warrant apologies. It should be celebrated.

'I've never felt like this before,' he murmured, resting his forehead against her hair.

'Me neither,' she whispered, because she couldn't lie. She felt the shudder that ran through him at her words, felt him tense after it had passed, and knew that he didn't believe her. He still didn't trust her or, worse still, didn't trust himself. He was afraid to rely on his instincts and believe they were genuine.

She cupped his face between her hands and looked into his eyes, praying that she could convince him. 'I've never felt this way with anyone except you, Vincenzo. It was the same when we first met. You…well, you made me feel things that I'd never felt for anyone before.'

'I find that very hard to believe,' he began roughly, but she stopped him the most expedient way she knew. Pressing her mouth to his, she kissed him, stopping the words even if she couldn't allay his doubts. He responded immediately, pulling her to him and kissing her with a hunger that made her heart soar. Maybe he wasn't convinced but he would be. In time and with patience.

When he let her go and took hold of her hand, Lowri knew what was coming next. She also knew that it was what she wanted for many reasons. She wanted to help Megan—that was a given. But she wanted this for herself as well, wanted to make love with him and feel like she had done five years ago in Milan.

Her breath caught because she had never allowed herself to think about how much she had benefited from what had happened then. Once she had realised she was pregnant, that had taken precedence. But now she could see how much she had gained from those weeks they had spent together. She had rediscovered herself during that time, changed from being the victim of a cruel trick to a woman who could cope with whatever life threw at her. Vincenzo had given her so much as well as her precious daughter. He had given her back her self-esteem.

Moonlight bathed the room with a silvery glow, lending a dreamlike quality to the familiar scene. Vincenzo held Lowri's hand as he closed the door and led her to the bed. It was the first time he had brought a woman to the villa since his divorce. And even when he had been married, Carla had spent very little time here. Carla had preferred the more hectic pace of city life so he had tended to visit the villa by himself. It had become a place to escape to, a place of respite from work and other pressures. It was the perfect place for him and Lowri to make love.

His heart jolted so hard that it felt as though it was going to leap right out of his chest. He took a deep breath as he sat her down on the bed and knelt in front of her. Now that the moment had arrived for them to make love, he was filled with fresh uncertainties. What if he failed to meet her expectations? What if she was disappointed by his lovemaking? He had never given any thought to his abilities as a lover before and yet all of a sudden he was afraid that he might not be able to satisfy her. He couldn't bear to think that she might look back on this night with revulsion.

'Don't.' Her voice was low, filled with understanding, and he sighed. There was no point trying to lie, no point at all trying to save face.

'I want tonight to be special, Lowri, but what if it isn't? What if you discover that you can't bear me touching you?'

'That isn't going to happen.' She bent and kissed him on the forehead, and her eyes were filled with all sorts of emotions, most of which he couldn't put a name to. The only one he did recognise was desire. He pulled her to him, not needing to see anything else. He wanted her and she wanted him—that was enough!

His heart was racing as he ran his hands down her back, urging her closer so that their bodies were melded together from throat to hip. He could feel the firm swell of her breasts pressing against him and groaned. Although he had slept with other women since he had slept with her, he didn't remember them. Even though the encounters had been pleasant enough, they had faded from his mind. However, he remembered how it had been with Lowri, remembered her softness, her womanliness; remembered how she had felt and how she had made him feel too.

All of a sudden it all came flooding back, their passion, her response, his need to give every tiny bit of himself and not hold anything back. He had never made love with anyone the way he had made love with her.

The thought shocked him, stunned him, made him see just how profound this moment really was. He would be making love to the only woman who had ever unlocked his emotions. His hands were shaking as he set her away from him. When he tried to unzip her dress, he discovered that he simply couldn't do it. His eyes rose to her face and he saw her smile, saw the tenderness that lit her eyes from within.

'Let me.'

Reaching behind her back, she slid the zipper down, the soft rasp of metal sounding so loud in the silence that Vincenzo jumped. He took a steadying breath, afraid that if he didn't get a grip he might lose it completely and that would never do. He needed this night, needed her in his arms, needed to hold her, love her, needed to feel like he had done all those years ago.

The thought unlocked all his inhibitions. Reaching out, he drew the straps of her dress off her shoulders and let it fall to her waist. She was wearing a pale pink bra beneath, the lacy cups doing little to conceal her breasts, and he sucked in another breath when he saw her nipples pushing proudly against the delicate fabric.

'You are so beautiful, *cara*. So very, very beautiful.'

The words tailed off because it was too hard to speak when he needed to absorb the picture she made, sitting here on his bed. He raised his hand, tracing the warm swell of her breasts with his fingertips, and heard her sigh. Bending, he placed his mouth over her nipple and drew it between his lips, his heart pounding when he heard her moan. He knew then that his fears were groundless, that whatever happened tonight would be even better than what had gone on before. Lowri wanted him. He wanted her. And it made no difference what their reasons were for mak-

ing love because it was going to be magical. Special.
Unforgettable. For him and for her.

Lowri could feel the blood drumming through her
veins as Vincenzo stripped off her dress then laid her
down on the bed. All she had on now were her bra
and panties and they were soon dispensed with. She
watched as he shed his own clothes, dropping them
in a careless heap on the floor. His body was lean
and fit, the muscles in his arms and chest flexing as
he lay down beside her. When she felt his hand start
to explore her body, she kept her eyes open, wanting
to see his face.

Did he remember how she had felt? she wondered.
Remember the dips and hollows, the texture of her
skin? She'd had a baby since then, so there were bound
to be changes, but did she feel familiar to him? Could
he recall their lovemaking in perfect, exquisite detail, as she could? She hoped so, she really did. If he
remembered how it had been that night then it must
have meant something to him.

The thought settled in her mind, stayed there as his
hand moved from her throat to her breasts and then
to her waist. It was the very lightest of touches, no
more than a ripple of skin floating across skin, and
yet she could feel her desire building. When he finally
reached the very core of her femininity, she was holding her breath, waiting for the moment when he would
explore there too. She had never felt this need before,
never felt it with anyone apart from Vincenzo…

The sound of a phone ringing sliced through the
silence and she jumped. Vincenzo's hand stilled, his
eyes flying to the heap of clothing on the floor.

'I don't believe this,' he muttered, swinging his legs over the side of the bed. Dragging his trousers from the pile, he found his phone and pressed it to his ear. *'Sì?'*

Lowri lay quite still, her heart aching and racing at the same time. Vincenzo was speaking on the phone and even though she couldn't understand what he was saying, it sounded urgent. She closed her eyes, stifling her disappointment because she had a bad feeling where this was leading.

'Sì. Sì. Subito!'

He ended the call and tossed the phone onto the bed. Lowri opened her eyes and looked at him in silence. He sighed as he scooped up his clothes and tossed them onto the bed as well.

'I have to leave. The condition of a patient I operated on this afternoon has deteriorated and I need to see him.' He zipped up his trousers then dragged his shirt over his head. 'It's a child—a young boy not much older than Megan. He is gravely ill, I'm afraid.'

'I understand.'

Lowri tried to speak calmly, tried her best not to let him see how she really felt, but knew she'd failed. He sat down on the bed and pulled her into his arms, holding her tightly against him.

'I am sorry, *cara*. I know how much this meant to you.'

'Do you?'

'Of course.' He tipped up her face and looked into her eyes. 'The sooner we can conceive this child, the better it will be for Megan. *Sì?*'

'Yes,' she agreed hollowly. Was that really all tonight had meant to him? Had he wanted to make love to her purely because of Megan? She didn't want to believe it was the only reason but she wasn't confident enough to dispute it.

'If it is at all possible then I shall come back later.' He frowned when she didn't reply. 'If that is what you want.'

'I don't want to put any pressure on you, Vincenzo,' she said flatly. She slid out of his arms, turning her back to him as she picked up her dress and slipped it over her head. 'I understand that your patient has to come first.'

'Do you?' He gave a small shrug as he picked up his shoes. 'Of course you do. You're a nurse and you must have found yourself in similar situations, I imagine.'

Not really, Lowri thought wryly, although it seemed easier to agree. 'Naturally. Don't worry if you can't make it back tonight. There will be other nights, I expect.'

'I expect there will.' His tone was cool. If he was disappointed that their plans had been scuppered, it certainly wasn't apparent.

Lowri's heart was heavy as she followed him from the room. She paused on the landing, knowing that she couldn't bear to go downstairs and see him off. Maybe it was of little consequence to him that they had been interrupted but she found it very hard to accept that tonight hadn't been special for him and that any other night would be equally as good.

'I'll check on Megan,' she told him, praying that he couldn't tell how her heart was aching. 'I hope it goes well, Vincenzo. For your patient, I mean.'

'*Grazie.*'

He gave her a quick smile then ran down the stairs. Lowri heard the front door open and a moment later the sound of a car starting up. She made her way to Megan's room, her hand shaking as she reached for the doorhandle. If the phone hadn't rung, she and Vincenzo would be making love this very minute. Would they have conceived a child tonight? She had no idea. There were no guarantees after all, nothing to say that it would have happened tonight or any other night. She would have to wait and see, although one thing was certain: when they did make love, it would be because of Megan and not for any other reason. Vincenzo had made that perfectly clear.

Vincenzo did his best, employing every scrap of the skill he had gained over the years, but it still wasn't enough. Little Giorgio died on the operating table and all that was left for him to do was to break the news to his parents.

They were heartbroken, their grief so palpable that Vincenzo felt moved almost beyond bearing. It wasn't the first time he'd had to break bad news to relatives and it wouldn't be the last time either, he knew. However, the child's death had affected him far more than he had expected. He couldn't help thinking about Megan and how he would feel if some doctor came and gave him equally terrible news. The thought brought tears to his eyes and he was hard pressed to contain them.

'I am so very sorry,' he repeated. 'If there was anything more I could have done...'

He broke off, knowing how pointless it was telling them that. It wouldn't change the outcome and that was all they cared about. He excused himself and left them clinging together for comfort, feeling more downhearted than he had felt in his entire life. He would have given anything to change the outcome but it simply wasn't possible.

'Are you OK?' Jack Wallace had been with him in Theatre and had gone with him to speak to Giorgio's parents. Vincenzo saw the look Jack gave him and sighed. Obviously, it was a shock for his registrar to discover that he felt anything for his patients.

'Losing a patient is always difficult,' he said neutrally.

He punched the button for the lift, willing it to come. The last thing he needed was an in-depth examination of his feelings tonight of all nights. His heart jolted painfully as he recalled the bleakness on Lowri's face when he had left her. Why hadn't he made it clear that he regretted what had happened, that he wished with all his heart they hadn't been interrupted? All it would have taken were a few words of reassurance yet he had found himself unable to say anything. He'd felt too upset, too vulnerable, too damned *everything* to admit how devastated he had been! He slammed his hand against the button again in a fit of impatience and heard Jack sigh.

'It's rotten when something like this happens. It always makes me feel as though I should have done something more but it isn't always possible. The kid was in such a bad way when he was admitted that it's a wonder he survived so long. I sometimes wonder if it would be kinder all round if we didn't attempt the impossible.'

Vincenzo knew it was true, knew that every word

his registrar said was correct, but it didn't help. He rounded on the younger man, his eyes blazing. 'If that's what you think then I pity your patients,' he snarled. 'We're here to save lives, not to stand aside and let people die.'

'That wasn't what I meant,' Jack protested. 'I firmly believe that we should do all we can, but some-times—like in this instance—you know it isn't going to work. It just seems wrong to raise the parents' hopes like that.'

'Maybe. But if it was your child then you would feel very differently, I assure you. You'd want to be sure that everything possible was done for your child.' His voice caught because he couldn't help thinking about Megan and what he would want for her, what he would *do* for her, in fact. He would happily give up his own life if it meant she would survive.

The thought was just too profound. Vincenzo knew that he couldn't deal with it and carry on a conversa-tion. Swinging round, he headed for the stairs, uncar-ing what the younger man thought. What did it matter what anyone thought about him? It was Megan who mattered; her health was the most important thing of all. He was her father. He had helped to bring her into this world and it was his duty to protect her. No mat-ter what it took, no matter how hard it was for him, he was going to do that!

CHAPTER ELEVEN

LOWRI HAD JUST finished giving Megan her breakfast when she heard a car coming up the drive. She walked to the end of the terrace but she couldn't see the vehicle from there. She went back to the table and wiped Megan's mouth. It was probably a delivery van and Alfredo would deal with it.

'*Buon giorno*. How are you this morning, *tesoro*?'

She jumped when Vincenzo appeared. She hadn't expected him to drive all the way back to the villa so early and it was a shock to see him, not a particularly pleasant one either. She dredged up a smile, not wanting him to suspect that she had a problem about his being there. Maybe last night hadn't meant as much to him as it had done to her, but she had to get over it if she wanted to help Megan.

'I wasn't expecting you back so soon,' she said coolly, helping Megan down from her chair.

'No?' His dark brows rose mockingly. 'I did say I would be back.'

Megan ran over to him, grabbing hold of his hand to lead him into the garden, so they didn't get a chance to say anything else, not that Lowri was disappointed.

Maybe she was mistaken but there'd been a definite hint of something...*dangerous* in his voice just now.

She shrugged off the thought, knowing how foolish it was. Loading the dishes onto a tray, she took them into the kitchen. Maria had arrived early and was busy making bread dough so she stacked them in the dishwasher, shaking her head when the housekeeper protested. While she appreciated everything that Maria did for them, she didn't want to get too used to being looked after. Once she returned home, she would have to do everything herself, cook and clean as well as take care of Megan and the new baby. Assuming there was going to be a baby.

Panic overwhelmed her. If she didn't have this child and something happened to Megan then she would never forgive herself. She had to go ahead, had to give Megan the chance of living a long and happy life. And if that meant sleeping with Vincenzo that's what she would do, even if she knew that it meant nothing to him. She had to set aside her scruples for the sake of her daughter. Surely that was enough to keep her strong, enough to stop her wishing for more. Maybe Vincenzo didn't love her, maybe he didn't care very much either, but if he helped to save Megan then she would be eternally grateful to him.

Vincenzo spent the morning allowing himself to be led around. Megan showed him all her favourite places, insisting that he crawl under this bush or look under that rock in the hope that they would find some kind of small treasure. It was a whole new experience for him to be involved in her games and he discovered to his surprise how much he was enjoying himself. It made him see that he was very different from his own father.

It was a revelation to realise it. Vincenzo knew that he needed to think about it but it was hard to do that when Megan kept demanding he play with her. When Lowri announced that it was time for the child to take a nap, he went to his study and sat down at his desk so he could think it all through.

He had always believed that he was exactly like his father in many respects. Umberto Lombardi had been a cold and distant man who had cared little for others, even his own son. He had been more interested in making money so as soon as he could he had sent Vincenzo away to school. They'd had very little contact after that and although Vincenzo hadn't missed him, his father's indifference had had a huge influence on him.

He had grown up expecting very little from other people. Although he had a few friends, there was nobody close to him. He preferred it that way. He was self-contained, focused, single-minded when it came to his career. He had known what he'd wanted to achieve and had gone after it with ruthless determination. Up till now. Now everything had changed. He could no longer put his own interests first. Not now there was Megan to consider. And Lowri.

He got up from the desk and went to the window. Having Lowri reappear in his life had turned it upside down. Whereas before he had been content with the way he lived, he wasn't content any longer. He wanted more than this sterile existence! He wanted to grab life by the throat and live it to the full. And if that meant falling in love, getting married, having a family, well, he wanted them too.

His head spun because the idea was so mind-blowing. He wanted to fall in love, wanted to be a husband and a father, but could he do it? Was he capable of being both or either of those things?

He wished he knew, wished there were guarantees, certainties, but there weren't. All he knew was that if he didn't take this chance, he might never get another one. He most certainly wouldn't get the chance to spend his life with Lowri, that was sure. And that was what he wanted more than anything.

It was the strangest of days. On the surface it appeared as though everything was flowing smoothly but Lowri was too aware of the undercurrents to let that fool her. Vincenzo didn't put a foot wrong all day. He played with Megan, showing endless patience as the little girl involved him in all her games. He was the epitome of the perfect host when they all had lunch together, too, asking questions about Lowri's life and seemingly fascinated by her answers. When Megan had her nap, he suggested they should make use of the time to swim in the pool.

Although Lowri agreed, it was more for politeness' sake than anything else. Quite frankly, she found it unnerving to be subjected to such a blatant charm offensive. What did he want? What was he planning? She wished she knew.

By the time evening fell her nerves were stretched to breaking point. Megan had worn herself out so once she had eaten her supper, Lowri put her to bed. She lingered upstairs as long as she could but in the end knew that she couldn't put off the moment any longer. Maria was waiting to serve dinner before she left and it wasn't fair to delay her.

Vincenzo was in the *salone* when she went downstairs. He looked round and smiled when she appeared but once again Lowri could feel the tension in the air and her heart gave a nervous little hiccup. He was up to something—she'd put good money on it too! But what exactly? That was the question.

'I thought we'd have a drink in here before dinner. There's a storm brewing so we won't be able to eat outside tonight.'

'Really?' Lowri went to the window and stared out. She gave a little shrug. 'It looks quite calm to me.'

'You get to know the signs when you live here for any length of time,' he said smoothly. He poured some wine into a crystal glass and brought it over to her. He handed her the glass then pointed to the mountains. 'You can see the clouds gathering over there. It looks as though we're in for some really rough weather.'

Lowri barely glanced at the lowering sky. She was far too conscious of his nearness to worry about climatic changes. She took a gulp of her wine and coughed when it shot down the wrong way.

'Careful!' Taking the glass off her, he patted her on the back but it didn't help. If anything, it made it worse. Now she not only had to contend with the spasm in her throat but his touch as well.

She shook her head, gasping for air. 'Don't!'

'*Mi scusi.*' He stepped back, his face immediately closing up. By the time that she had finally managed to drag some air into her aching lungs, he had moved away and was pouring himself a glass of wine. She sighed, very aware that she had overreacted.

'Sorry. I didn't mean to snap at you.'

'It doesn't matter.' He gave a small shrug as he sat down. To all intents and purposes, it appeared that he was telling the truth and that it didn't matter but she had seen the hurt in his eyes and felt guiltier than ever. There had been no need to react like that when he had been trying to help her.

'No, but I'm still sorry.' She bit her lip then rushed on, knowing that she had to say what was on her mind. 'I may be wrong but has something happened, Vincenzo?'

'I'm not sure I understand what you mean,' he countered, swirling the wine around his glass.

'It's just that you seem…well, different. I've noticed a certain undercurrent today and I'm not sure what the reason is for it. So has something happened?'

'Not that I'm aware of,' he began, but she held up her hand.

'Please! I know something's going on so there's no point lying. It would be easier if you told me the truth.'

'Perhaps. But I'm not sure if you really want to hear it.' He put down his glass and looked at her. Lowri felt her heart surge into her throat when she saw how serious he looked.

'Is…is it to do with Megan?' she asked, her voice catching so that the words sounded thin and shaky when they emerged.

'*Sì*. Megan. And you and this baby we may or may not have.'

'Have you changed your mind about the baby? Last night you seemed so certain it was what you wanted...' She tailed off, not wanting to think about what had so nearly happened the night before.

'No. I haven't changed my mind. But I have decided that I need to make some changes about what happens in the future,' he said flatly.

'What sort of changes?' she whispered, her heart racing. If they hadn't been interrupted by that phone call, they would have made love and the baby might even now be a reality.

'I want to be involved in both Megan's and the baby's lives but I can't do that unless you agree.' He took a deep breath then looked at her. 'Will you, Lowri? Will you let me be a proper father to our children?'

Vincenzo realised he was holding his breath but it was too hard to do anything as complicated as breathe. His lungs were burning from the lack of oxygen and still Lowri didn't answer.

'Why?' Her voice was so low that he wasn't sure if she had actually spoken or not. He answered anyway, wanting—*needing*—to make her understand how much it meant to him.

'Because I don't want to walk away. I want to be involved, want to watch them growing up, want to be there to help and to guide them.'

'But you told me that you had never wanted a family.'

'And it was true—I never did. But everything has changed—*I've* changed. I've realised that I can't just disappear from their lives and leave you to bring them up on your own. I want to help. If you will let me.'

Vincenzo could feel the tension that had gripped him all day gathering momentum as he willed her to give him the answer he wanted so desperately. He wanted to be a real father to his children, wanted it so badly that he ached, but would she agree? After all, it would mean him being part of her life too and he wasn't sure if that was what she wanted. Lowri might not want him, even though he wanted her. Desperately.

The thought stunned him. Oh, he had skirted around it for days, let it flit in and out of his mind like a butterfly, always hovering and never settling. Now he realised exactly what it meant and the truth was so shocking that he had trouble grasping it.

He was falling in love with her. He might even have started falling in love with her five years ago, only that idea was a step too far and he couldn't deal with it. He wanted her in his life not only because she was the mother of his children but because he couldn't imagine a future without her.

His head reeled yet, oddly, he didn't feel afraid. Although he had spent his adult life avoiding emotional entanglements, he wasn't going to shy away any more. He was capable of loving a woman if that woman was her.

He stood up, holding her gaze as he crossed the room. She was standing so still that she looked as though she had been frozen in place. It had been a shock for her too, he knew, but she would deal with it in her own way. She was brave and strong and he couldn't think of anyone he admired more.

He took her hands and drew her to him, kissed her lightly on the lips and then stepped back. He might want to sweep her into his arms and carry her up to his bed, but he knew it would be wrong to rush her.

She had to decide what she wanted. And he had to give her the time and the space to do it too.

'I don't expect an answer right away,' he said softly. 'You need to think about it and I understand that. But I mean what I say, Lowri. I want to be a proper father to Megan and this baby.'

'I don't know what to say.' She looked at him and he could see the bewilderment in her eyes. 'I never expected you would feel this way, Vincenzo.'

'Neither did I.' He kissed her again then glanced round when Maria appeared to tell them dinner was ready. They were eating in the dining room and he led the way, pulling out a chair for Lowri. There were candles on the table, their flickering light bouncing off the crystal and silverware, casting shadows over her face so that he couldn't read her expression. He sighed regretfully as he took his seat because he needed all the help he could get. Would she agree or would she refuse? It was impossible to tell.

By the time the meal ended, Vincenzo felt as though he was teetering on the edge of an abyss. Lowri still hadn't told him if she would agree to his request and the wait was becoming unbearable. It was one thing to decide to give her time and another thing entirely to have to live through it, he realised ruefully. When Maria came to see if she should serve coffee in the *salone*, he barely managed to curb his impatience.

'*Sì. Grazie,* Maria.' He stood up, tossing his linen napkin onto the table. Lowri stood up as well and he smiled at her, falling back on good manners to see him through this most stressful night in his entire life. 'Coffee?'

'No, thank you.' She walked around the table, pausing when she drew level with him. Her eyes were very clear and his breath caught because there was no doubt about the message they were conveying. 'I think I'll go straight up to bed.'

She left the room, not waiting for him to say anything. There was no need. They both knew what was going to happen, that tonight they were going to make love. Was that her answer? he wondered as he went into the *salone* and poured himself a cup of coffee. Was she telling him that she agreed to him playing a part in their children's lives? He hoped so, he really did, because if it were true it meant that he could be part of her life as well.

His hands shook as put the cup back on the tray. He didn't want coffee. He wanted Lowri. Tonight and for evermore.

Lowri could feel her heart racing as she stepped out of her dress. She hung it up then took a nightdress out of the drawer. The cotton felt cool against her skin and she shivered. Was she doing the right thing? Should she agree to Vincenzo's request when it would have major repercussions for her? After all, if he was to be a proper father to Megan and the baby, he would be a part of her life too.

The thought made her head swim and she went to the window, hoping the fresh air would help to alleviate her dizziness. The light had faded now and the sky was black with storm clouds. As she watched, lightning flashed across the sky, a brilliant bolt of light that momentarily dazzled her. She closed her eyes, seeing the imprint of it on her retinas, one bright clear flash in the midst of all the darkness, exactly like the thought that shot into her mind: she couldn't imagine a future without Vincenzo.

The sound of the door opening made her glance round and she felt her heart fill with all sorts of emotions when she saw him come into the room. When she had decided to approach him and ask for his help, she hadn't thought about the impact it would have on her. Oh, she had expected it to be…awkward. After all, he hadn't replied to her letter, so she'd had no great hope that he would agree to her request but she had refused to let that deter her. She had been willing to do anything, suffer any embarrassment if it meant she could help Megan.

Now she could see how naïve she had been to imagine that she could conceive and carry a child and not feel anything for its father. It hadn't happened with Megan. Even though she had tried to blot out all thoughts of Vincenzo when she had been pregnant, she hadn't succeeded. She had thought about him all the time, remembered how good those weeks they'd had together had been. Why? Because it was what pregnant women did? Or because she had fallen in love with him?

She had always denied that possibility, to herself and to Cerys too, but she had been lying. She had fallen in love with Vincenzo in Milan and that was why she had wanted to have his baby, why she had been so hurt when she'd thought he had ignored her; it was why she had been willing to have another child with him too.

Thoughts flashed through her mind, so bright and clear that she knew they were true. When Vincenzo came and took her in his arms, her heart ached. He might have asked to be part of their children's lives but he hadn't said anything about wanting to be part of her life and she must never forget that. Just because she loved him, it didn't mean that he loved her too.

Tears stung her eyes as he bent and kissed her but she blinked them away, not wanting anything to spoil this moment. Maybe he didn't love her and never would but he wanted her—that was obvious. Wrapping her arms around his neck, she drew him to her, her lips parting so he could deepen the kiss, and felt him shudder. And it was a small consolation to know that his need for her was so great. At least she had unlocked his emotions and that had to count for something.

Lifting her into his arms, he carried her to the bed and laid her down. He knelt beside her, taking hold of her hand so he could press his lips to her palm. Lowri shuddered, feeling her desire take flight. She wanted this so much and for so many reasons.

'The answer is yes, Vincenzo,' she said softly. 'If you want to be a proper father to Megan and any other child we may have then I agree.'

'Thank you, *cara*.' Tears filmed his eyes and the sight of them moved her beyond bearing. Maybe he didn't love her but he would love their children and that was enough.

When he stripped off her nightdress, she helped him, helped him strip off his own clothes too. Lightning flashed across the sky, lighting the room and turning their skin to burnished silver as they lay entwined in one another's arms. Lowri closed her eyes when she felt his hands begin to explore her body. She wanted to savour every touch, each caress, store them all up so she could look back on this night. It might not happen again. Vincenzo might neither need nor want to make love to her again but she would have her memories and she would treasure them too. This was the night she had realised that she loved him and it was precious, special. A night she would never forget no matter what happened in the future. And if they conceived a child tonight, it would be even more perfect.

Thunder rolled across the sky as he entered her, the noise filling her head as Vincenzo filled her body, and finally she let her tears fall. This might be all she had, this one magical turbulent night in his arms.

CHAPTER TWELVE

VINCENZO LAY IN the darkness and listened as the storm receded. It had started raining now, the raindrops beating against the open window and spattering the marble floor. He really should get up and close it, he thought, but he couldn't bear to get out of bed and bring an end to the most profound experience of his life. Making love to Lowri had been everything he had dreamt it would be and a lot more too.

He sighed as he rolled onto his side and looked at her as she lay sleeping beside him. How would she feel if he admitted that he loved her? Would she be pleased, sorry, disbelieving even? After all, she had no reason to trust him. He had failed to reply to her letter—a letter he had never received, he amended to appease his conscience—so why should she believe him if he declared his feelings? She might think it was some sort of a ruse he had dreamed up for his own nefarious reasons, and he couldn't bear that.

He didn't want her to doubt him, to possibly reconsider her decision to let him be involved in the children's lives. It might be better if he said nothing rather than run the risk of that happening.

'I hope I wasn't snoring.'

He fixed a smile to his lips when he realised she was awake. Although it would be difficult to hide his feelings, he had to think about the bigger picture. And, hopefully, the time would come when he could be honest with her. If it didn't then he would just have to deal with it. After all, he was an expert when it came to bottling up his feelings.

'Just a very gentle snore,' he said, trying not to dwell on the thought that it would be far harder to curb his emotions now they'd had a taste of freedom. He ran his hand down her arm, feeling a shiver dance across her skin at his touch. It was so entrancing that he did it again, his body immediately stirring to life as his fingers skated over the warm, smooth flesh. It made no difference that they had made love until they'd both been exhausted: he still wanted her.

'Really? Oh, no, how embarrassing!' She raised herself up on her elbow and grimaced. 'Although it could have been worse. I might have been drooling!'

'Did I say you weren't?' He laughed when she gasped. Taking hold of her hand, he pulled her down into his arms. 'I was teasing you, *cara*. Forgive me.'

'On one condition,' she said severely, holding him at bay with a hand pressed against his chest.

'And that is?'

'That I receive a suitably heartfelt apology.'

'Oh, I think I can manage that,' he growled, quickly dispensing with the gap between them.

He kissed her passionately, his desire surging when he felt her kiss him back. They made love and once again it was so moving that Vincenzo couldn't hold back. Maybe he couldn't tell her in words how he felt, but he could show her through their lovemaking. And maybe, just maybe, she would start to believe him.

Lowri could feel every tiny bit of her suffused with love as Vincenzo kissed her. Could he feel it too, she wondered, feel all the emotions that filled the air and made what was happening so special? She thought he could but it was hard to be sure. Perhaps she was read-ing more into it than actually existed and the thought sent a chill through her. She wanted him to love her as much as she loved him but she had to accept that it might never happen.

When he fell asleep, she lay and watched him, stor-ing up more memories for the future. Oh, he would be part of her life but he wouldn't be the linchpin, merely a visitor. He would come to see Megan and the baby and, by necessity, see her too, but their relation-ship wouldn't progress beyond that. It wasn't what he wanted, as he had made clear.

The thought stayed with her as night faded. Lowri got up when the sun started to rise. Going into the bathroom, she stood under the shower and let the hot water wash away all her foolish dreams. She knew what she had to do, how she had to behave, and she wouldn't embarrass Vincenzo by letting him know how she felt. It would be her secret to be kept locked away in her heart.

It was only when she went back into the bedroom and saw him lying in the bed that she realised how hard it was going to be. How could she hope to hide her feelings if she was living in his house? She wasn't that good an actress and he would soon suspect something was wrong. It left just one course open to her: she would have to leave the villa.

By the time he woke, Lowri was dressed and standing by the window. The storm had wreaked havoc in the garden and Alfredo was clearing up. Her heart was heavy as she watched him push his wheelbarrow across the lawn. Maybe she would visit the villa again at some point but it would be very different then. She had discovered her love for Vincenzo here and had lost it here too. She could imagine how difficult it would be to come back and recall what had happened last night.

'*Buon giorno.* Did you sleep well?'

'Very well, thank you.' She fixed a smile to her mouth as she turned, determined to start as she meant to continue. Vincenzo must never suspect how hard it was to pretend that she didn't care. 'The storm didn't bother me in the least.'

'That is good to hear.'

He tossed back the sheet and she averted her eyes. She didn't want to look at his beautiful body and remember what had happened or she might not be able to stick to her decision. When he came over to her, she steeled herself. It would need so little to weaken her resolve and she couldn't bear it if he guessed how she felt. Not when he didn't feel the same way.

'Are you all right, *cara*?' He bent and looked at her in concern. 'You seem very subdued this morning. Nothing is wrong, I hope?'

'Of course not. Why should anything be wrong? We achieved what we set out to do, didn't we?' Her smile was meaningless, mere window dressing for the

rebuff, and her heart ached when she saw him immediately draw back.

'We did indeed. Now, if you'll excuse me, I shall
get dressed. I shall see you at breakfast.'

Gathering up his clothes, he left the room, the very
stiffness of his posture telling her that he had taken
her words to heart. Tears filled her eyes but she knew
that she didn't dare give in to them. She had to stay
strong, had to do whatever was necessary. It would
be intolerable if Vincenzo realised that she was in
love with him. He would feel highly uncomfortable
about maintaining contact with Megan and the baby,
so much so that he might decide not to see them at
all. The thought that her actions could have a detrimental effect on them was more than she could bear.

Her hand went to her stomach. For Megan's sake
and for the sake of the baby she might even now be
carrying, she couldn't allow that to happen.

Vincenzo showered and dressed, wondering what he
should do. There was no doubt in his mind that Lowri
had been very offhand with him. After their close-
ness the previous night, he found her withdrawal all
the more difficult to understand. Had he done something to upset her? But what?

By the time he went downstairs, his head was
whirling. It was hard to summon a smile when Megan
came running over as he stepped out onto the terrace.

'*Buon giorno,*' she said, laughing up at him.

'*Buon giorno, tesoro.*' Vincenzo tried to shrug off
his unease, determined not to let the little girl see
that he was upset. It wasn't Megan's fault, after all. 'I

see that you are learning Italian. What a clever girl you are.'

He bent and dropped a kiss on the top of her head then straightened when he heard footsteps behind him. He didn't need to look to know they belonged to Lowri; his heart had already warned him. He sighed as he turned to face her, wondering how he was going to cope. It wouldn't be easy to hide his feelings but he would have to do so if he wanted to maintain contact with Megan. Lowri certainly wouldn't appreciate him visiting them and laying bare his soul!

'Good morning again. It's a beautiful morning too after that storm.' His tone was polite to a fault and he saw her eyes darken before she turned away.

'It is. The storm seems to have cleared the air, doesn't it?' She placed the basket of rolls she was carrying on the table then called Megan over and got her seated.

Vincenzo took his place, wondering if there was any reason to hope that she wasn't as indifferent to him as she had appeared. He sighed softly as he helped himself to coffee. He was clutching at straws and it had to stop. He had to accept that Lowri didn't love him and that last night had been special purely because it had been the culmination of all her hopes for saving Megan. If she'd wanted him, it had been for that reason and none other.

The realisation hit him hard. It was all he could do not to show how devastated he felt. Fortunately, Megan was unaffected by his downbeat mood and chattered on. When she begged him to take her for a trip on one of the ferries, he agreed with alacrity.

Anything to get him out of the house and away from Lowri seemed like a wonderful idea.

He sent Megan upstairs to fetch her jacket and stood up. Glancing at Lowri, he shrugged. 'If we go now, we shall avoid the worst of the crowds. It will be better for Megan.'

'Of course.' She hesitated then hurried on. 'I've decided to return home. Staying here has done Megan the world of good, but it's time we went back to England.'

'If that's what you want to do, I won't try to stop you,' he replied quietly, his heart aching. It was obvious that she couldn't wait to leave now that her plan had reached fruition, and the thought merely reinforced everything he had been thinking. Lowri hadn't wanted *him* last night; she had wanted what he could give her. Another child.

'When were you thinking of leaving?' he asked, praying that she couldn't tell that his heart was breaking.

'As soon as I can arrange a flight.' She shrugged. 'It's a busy time of the year so it could take a few days to get seats. I'll contact the airlines and see what's available.'

'There is no need to do that.' He dredged up a smile that seemed to have been dragged up from the very depths of his being. 'I'm returning to Milan after lunch so I shall get everything organised from there. It will be much safer for Megan if I hire a plane to fly you back.'

'Oh, I didn't realise you were going back to Milan today.'

'*Sì*. There is no point me staying any longer when

we have achieved our objective.' His smile was cool but it wasn't difficult to appear cold-hearted when it felt as though every bit of him had been turned to ice. 'You will let me know if you are pregnant, I assume.'

'I…erm… Of course.'

'*Grazie*. And if it hasn't happened this time…'

'Let's worry about that once we find out,' she said hurriedly.

Picking up the bread basket, she disappeared inside, leaving Vincenzo alone with his thoughts. He sighed as he waited for Megan to return. He didn't want to think about how hard it was going to be if Lowri wasn't pregnant. Knowing that she was only making love with him for the sake of their daughter wasn't something he wanted to contemplate. Admittedly, he had agreed to her plan on that basis but everything had changed. Now that he knew how much he loved her, it would be unbearable to have to make love with her, knowing that she cared nothing for him.

Tilting back his head, he stared at the sky, praying that he would find the strength to do whatever was necessary. He had to forget how he felt and concentrate on Megan.

If he could.

It was one of the worst days Lowri could remember and she'd had more than her share of bad days since Megan had been taken ill. She set about packing their belongings with a heavy heart. Vincenzo had phoned to say that he and Megan were having lunch in Malcesine so at least that gave her a breathing space, not that it helped very much. She loved Vincenzo and there was nothing she could do about it, the same as there was nothing she could do about the fact that he didn't love her. She had to live with the situation but she knew it was going to be difficult, especially if it did turn out that she was pregnant.

As she piled clothes into their cases, she tried not to think about the future and how hard it was going to be to hide her feelings when he came to visit them. It would be a huge strain but she didn't have a choice. She was going to have to learn to present a neutral front no matter how painful she found it.

By the time Vincenzo and Megan returned it was almost two. Lowri could tell at once that Megan was exhausted and took her upstairs for a nap. She got her settled then went downstairs, knowing that she couldn't avoid speaking to Vincenzo even though it was what she wanted to do. She squared her shoulders before she knocked on the study door. She could only hope it would get easier in time.

'*Sì?*' He was reading through some papers when she went in. He looked up and Lowri felt her heart turn over. He looked so sombre that for a moment she found herself wondering if he was having as hard a time hiding his feelings as she was. It was only when she saw one brow arch quizzically as she continued to stand there that she realised how foolish she was. If Vincenzo appeared to be somewhat subdued it was because he had something on his mind; it had nothing to do with her.

'I just wanted to let you know that I'm all packed. Is it all right if Megan takes some of those toys you bought for her? She's very attached to one of the dolls in particular and I know she'll be upset if she has to leave it behind.'

'She can take the whole lot,' he said gruffly. He tossed the papers onto the desk and stood up. 'Do you want me to arrange a flight for tomorrow or is that too soon?'

'No, that will be perfect.' She dredged up a smile. 'The sooner I get her home and back into her routine, the better.'

'Are you planning on returning to work immediately?'

'Yes.' She shrugged. 'Megan is much better so there's no reason for me to take any more time off. It's not fair to the people I work with.'

'Is it fair to Megan, though? Surely it would be better for her if you were there to look after her?'

Lowri bridled at the criticism. 'Megan understands that I need to work. She's used to me not being there all the time.'

'It still seems wrong that you are going to abandon her,' he said bluntly.

'I am not abandoning her!' she said hotly. 'Cerys will look after her the same as she has always done.'

'And look what happened the last time you left her with your sister. The poor child ended up in hospital. Maybe you should think about that.'

His tone was condemnatory. Lowri reared back, stunned by the fact that he was blaming her for what had happened. 'What I decide to do is up to me, Vincenzo. I need to work to provide for Megan—put a roof over her head and food on the table. Sadly, we don't all have your resources to fall back on.'

'Maybe not but I am willing to cover your expenses for however long it is necessary.' He came around the desk, stopping when he drew level with her, and

Lowri had to stop herself stepping back. His expression was so cold that it was hard to believe he was the same man who had held her in his arms the night before and aroused her passion to previously undiscovered heights.

'I will make you an allowance, more than enough money to pay your bills and ensure that you and Megan want for nothing.' He shrugged. 'If it does turn out that you are pregnant then you will need to stop work at some point so it may as well be sooner rather than later.'

If he had showed even the tiniest hint of emotion, it might have helped. She might even have considered the idea, although Lowri doubted if she would have agreed. The last thing she had ever wanted from him was money and she couldn't begin to explain how hurt and insulted she felt that he should believe she would accept his offer.

'Thank you but the answer is still no. I don't want your money, Vincenzo. I never have.'

She swung round and made for the door, pausing when he said quietly behind her, 'At least think about it. It makes sense, Lowri. I have the money and I am more than willing to pay my share.'

'No.' She glanced back, feeling tears burning her eyes. She loved him so much but all she was to him was a problem that needed solving. If he gave her money then it would mean he wouldn't need to give her anything else.

A sob welled to her throat and she spun round, wanting to escape before she made a fool of herself. Vincenzo didn't try to stop her as she crossed the hall and that seemed like an indictment in itself.

Why would he want to stop her after all? He didn't care about her, not really, not the woman she was, the woman he had held in his arms, kissed and caressed. He had slept with her for the sake of their daughter, so they could conceive another child and, hopefully, save Megan's life. Maybe he had enjoyed the experience to a point but at the end of the day it had been sex and nothing more.

Lowri made it to her room before the tears fell. She had cried many times in the past year, cried out of fear for Megan and the future, but this was different. This time she was crying for herself, for what she'd had so briefly and what she would never have again. Even if it did turn out that she wasn't pregnant, she couldn't go through this a second time, couldn't bear to have Vincenzo make love to her knowing that he felt nothing for her. Not even for Megan's sake could she do it. And that thought was the most bitter of all.

At the end of the day, she might not be strong enough to save her precious daughter.

CHAPTER THIRTEEN

'LUCKY YOU! I'D give *anything* to have a holiday at Lake Garda!'

'Yes, I am lucky.' Lowri managed to smile, although it wasn't easy to appear upbeat when it felt as though her heart was breaking. She had been back home for over a week and had hoped that distance might help to kick-start the healing process but it didn't seem to be working. She felt as emotionally raw as she had done when Vincenzo had seen them off at the airport.

She blanked out the thought, knowing that she couldn't think about him without bursting into tears. She had returned to work that day and it wasn't fair to her co-workers to be moping around the place. 'It was a lovely break but it's back to reality now. What's been happening here?'

'Oh, it's been the usual madhouse,' Amy told her wryly. 'Too many patients and not enough staff...' She broke off and grimaced. 'Sorry! I wasn't trying to lay a guilt trip on you.'

'I know.' Lowri sighed. 'I take it that you didn't get much cover while I was off?'

'We didn't get any. According to Eileen Roberts

there was "nobody suitable" on the agency's books.'
Amy emphasised the nursing manager's words by
making speech marks with her fingers.

Lowri groaned. 'That old chestnut. I don't believe
they haven't anyone on their books who's worked in
PICU.'

'Apparently not.' Amy shrugged. 'Still, we mud-
dled through and now that you're back, life should get
back to normal—whatever normal is!'

Lowri laughed dutifully as the staff nurse went to
check on a monitor that had started beeping. It was
good to know that she had been missed, although
she couldn't help feeling guilty about her colleagues
having to pick up her share of the workload. Still, she
was back now and it should make life easier for everyone, assuming that she didn't need to take more
time off soon.

She dismissed the thought, not wanting to explore
the reasons why she might need to take any more time
off. The break had done Megan good and her health
had improved dramatically, so much so that Lowri had
felt far more confident about leaving her that morning. She picked up the patient list, trying not to let
her mind race ahead. It was too soon to know if she
was pregnant so there was no point worrying about
that. If she was then she would deal with it and if she
wasn't…well, she would deal with that too.

The thought of how she would deal with that even-
tuality was more than she could handle and she pushed
it out of her mind. There had been a new admission
during the night and she went to check on him.

Nine-year-old Alfie Cullum had been admitted
with sepsis, a life-threatening condition caused by

the rapid multiplication of bacteria and the presence of toxins in the blood. It appeared that Alfie had cut his foot on some coral while he'd been visiting his grandparents in Australia and although the cut had been cleaned and dressed, it had become infected. He was receiving intravenous antibiotics and fluids, which would help to support him, but he was a very sick little boy. Lowri knew the next twenty-four hours were crucial.

His parents were with him so once she had introduced herself she answered their questions as best she could. Naturally enough, they wanted to know if he would get better but it was impossible to give a definite answer. If Alfie developed septic shock then the prognosis wasn't nearly as good.

'The main thing is that you brought him in as soon as you realised how ill he was,' she told them gently.

'I should have brought him even sooner,' Deborah Cullum declared, wiping her eyes with a tissue. 'I knew he wasn't right but we were all so tired after the journey and I kept telling myself it was that.'

'It's difficult to tell for sure with children,' Lowri assured her, sighing inwardly. She couldn't count the number of times that she, too, had blamed herself when Megan had developed some sort of ailment. 'The important thing is that Alfie is receiving the treatment he needs. That will stand in his favour.'

'I hope so. I don't know what I'll do if anything happens to him.'

Deborah started to sob. Lowri patted her shoulder and left the couple to console each other. She sighed as she went to check on the rest of her young charges. At least Alfie's parents had each other and that made

a huge difference. Having gone through the trauma of
Megan's illness on her own, she knew how hard it was.

If only Vincenzo had been there, it would have
been so much easier, she found herself thinking before
she dismissed the idea. Vincenzo hadn't been there
and there was no point wishing that he had. Anyway,
she had coped as she would cope no matter what happened in the future. The one thing she must never do
was assume that Vincenzo was going to be around
whenever she needed him.

A week passed, and another, and Vincenzo still didn't
hear a word from Lowri. It was as though the minute
she had stepped onto the plane she had disappeared
from his life, and he missed her. He tried to take his
mind off how he was feeling by immersing himself
in his work but, strangely enough, it didn't help. Even
in the middle of the most complex surgery, he found
himself thinking about her—wondering how she was
and if she was pregnant—and it was disconcerting not
to be able to channel his thoughts as he had always
been able to do.

He was afraid of making a mistake and got into the
habit of asking Jack Wallace to join him in Theatre
on the pretext of furthering the younger man's experience. Jack was delighted and Vincenzo was relieved
that he didn't need to explain his real reason for wanting him there. He may have changed a lot in the past
few months but he had no intention of letting anyone
know just how vulnerable he was.

By the end of the third week, he realised that he
couldn't wait any longer. He needed to know if Lowri
was pregnant. He phoned her home and left a mes-

sage, asking her to call him back; however, by the time he left the hospital he still hadn't heard from her. He went back to his apartment and phoned her again, feeling his irritation mount when once again he got her answering machine. He left a curt message and hung up. It was obvious that she was avoiding him but why? Because she wasn't pregnant and couldn't face the thought of having to sleep with him again?

His heart ached. It was the only answer that made sense and he hated it, hated the thought that she had found his lovemaking so distasteful when it had been the most wonderful experience of his life. However, the difference was that he loved her and she didn't love him.

Lowri stared at the plastic stick in her hand. She had put off doing the pregnancy test but she couldn't avoid it any longer. Her period was late and that could mean only one thing.

She checked her watch but it would be another minute before the result appeared. Vincenzo had phoned her twice but she hadn't returned his calls. She had decided that it would be easier if she could tell him one way or the other if she was pregnant or not. After that, well, she had no idea what she was going to do. If she wasn't pregnant, could she really see herself sleeping with him again?

Letters suddenly appeared in the test stick's window but for a moment she couldn't make out what they said. She took a deep breath and made herself focus, her heart leaping when she saw the single word: pregnant. Sitting down abruptly on the edge of the bath, she closed her eyes as relief washed over her. She was pregnant and there was a very good chance that this baby she was carrying would help to save its sister's life. It was what she had prayed for and now all that was left to do was to tell Vincenzo.

Lowri left the bathroom, knowing that it would be better to get it over with immediately. He had a right to know and the fact that she wasn't looking forward to speaking to him was irrelevant. Maybe he didn't love her but he had done what she had asked of him and she owed him a lot.

She hurried to the stairs, her foot hovering over the first tread when she heard Megan calling her. 'I'll be there in a minute, darling,' she replied, wondering how Vincenzo would react to her news. Maybe he had agreed to help Megan but did he really want the added burden of another child? He had claimed that he wanted to be involved in the children's lives but what if it had been purely out of a sense of duty?

The thought was so painful that she failed to look where she was going. Her foot missed the step and she gasped when she felt herself pitch forward. She went tumbling down the stairs, cracking her head on the newel post at the bottom. Darkness descended and her last thought before she slid into unconsciousness was that Vincenzo might never know about the baby now.

Vincenzo was leaving Theatre when one of the nurses informed him that his secretary had phoned to say there was an urgent message for him. He sighed as he went into the office and picked up the phone. He had just spent the last six hours bent over the operating table and he could do without having to deal with another case.

'You have a message for me,' he said curtly when his secretary answered, then listened with mounting horror as she relayed the message: Lowri was hurt. She was in hospital and her sister thought he would want to know.

Vincenzo hung up, his stomach churning as he tried to absorb what he had heard, but it was too much to take in. All he knew was that Lowri was hurt and that he needed to be with her. Hurrying out of the office, he headed for the lifts, uncaring that he was still wearing theatre scrubs. With a bit of luck he would be able to get on the next flight to England. If he couldn't get a seat then he would hire a plane to get him there. And when he did see Lowri then he would do what he should have done weeks ago: he would tell her that he loved her!

'I wish you hadn't phoned him, Cerys. I know you meant well but...'

'Never mind the buts,' Cerys said firmly. She shook an admonishing finger at her. 'He needed to know what happened—end of story.'

'I suppose so,' Lowri conceded, although if she hadn't felt quite so sick then she might have argued the point. After all, why would Vincenzo want to know about the accident? It wasn't as though he cared about her.

The thought didn't make her feel any better. When Cerys went to make a cup of tea, she rested her head against the cushions, wondering what would happen now. Would Vincenzo phone to see how she was? Possibly. It all depended how annoyed he was about her not replying to his messages. She sighed. The thought of having to speak to him was more than she could handle at the moment so she decided not to worry about it. She would face it if and when it was necessary.

Thankfully, she had been kept in hospital for just one night while she had been monitored for concussion. Once it had been established that she hadn't suffered any serious damage, she had been sent home. Cerys had collected her and she had insisted on staying with her too despite Lowri's assurances that she could manage. Now it was a waiting game. She would have to wait and see if the fall would create problems for this baby she was carrying.

Her heart contracted as she laid her hand protectively on her stomach. She had spoken to the hospital's obstetrician who had been sympathetic but realistic: a fall like this could bring on a miscarriage and all Lowri could do was to wait and see what happened in the next few days. The thought that her carelessness might mean her losing the baby was unbearable but she had to face it, the same as she had to face up to what she was going do if she did miscarry. Could she sleep with Vincenzo again, knowing that he didn't love her?

It was all too much. Lowri closed her eyes when she felt tears threaten. There was no point crying. She would make her decision if and when it happened. Anyway, it wasn't only up to her, was it? It also depended on how Vincenzo felt. Pain rippled through her. He might be no more eager to try again than she was.

Vincenzo managed to get on a flight to Manchester Airport. As soon as he cleared customs, he headed for the taxi rank. He gave the driver Lowri's address, nodding when the man asked him if he realised how much it was going to cost to drive all the way to Liverpool. He didn't care about the expense: he just wanted to see Lowri.

By the time the cab drew up outside her home, he was beside himself with worry. He paid the driver and ran up the path and knocked on the door. He wasn't sure what he was going to do if she wasn't here. He would have to check out the local hospitals, he assumed, and the thought intensified his fear. He couldn't bear to imagine Lowri lying injured in a hospital bed and not being able to find her.

'Yes?'

Vincenzo spun round when the door opened. Just for a second his heart lifted before he realised that it wasn't Lowri. 'My name is Vincenzo Lombardi,' he began, and saw the woman's face clear.

'So you came after all.' She smiled as she stepped aside. 'Come in. I'm Lowri's sister, Cerys.'

'It is good to meet you,' he said formally, stepping inside. He looked round when he heard footsteps, smiling when Megan came hurtling down the hall. '*Buon giorno, tesoro*. How are you?'

'I'm all right but Mummy's got a sore head,' she informed him importantly. 'She fell down the stairs.'

'How awful,' he replied, bending to give her a hug. He straightened and turned to Cerys. 'May I see her?'

'Of course.' Cerys opened the sitting-room door and put a finger to her lips. 'She's having a nap so why don't you go in and sit with her until she wakes up?' She took hold of Megan's hand when the child went to follow him. 'Come on, sweetie. Let's go and make some cupcakes as a surprise for Mummy.'

Vincenzo closed the door as Cerys led Megan away. Crossing the room, he stared down at Lowri, his heart filling with so many emotions, most of which he hadn't believed himself capable of feeling. He loved her so much, needed her, wanted to spend the rest of his days with her, but would it happen?

Or was he destined to live his life on the perimeter of hers, a visitor who dipped in and out of her world at intervals but never occupied a real space? He couldn't bear to think that was all he might ever be but he had to face facts, and the most important fact of all was that Lowri didn't love him and there was no reason to think that she would.

Lowri awoke slowly, feeling disorientated as she always did if she fell asleep during the day. Easing herself up against the cushions, she looked around, surprised when she realised how late it was. If the clock on the mantelpiece was to be believed she must have slept for several hours.

'So, you are awake at last, *cara*. Good.'

The deep voice seemed to reverberate throughout the room and she jumped. Turning her head, she stared in shock at the figure standing by the window. He had his back to the light so that his face was in shadow but he sounded so like Vincenzo that for a moment she almost believed it was him until she realised that it was her imagination playing tricks. Vincenzo would never have flown all this way to see her; he didn't care enough. The thought brought a rush of tears to her eyes.

'Don't cry. I cannot bear to see you cry, my darling.'

He came and crouched in front of her, taking her hands in his, and Lowri felt another bolt of shock run through her when she felt him tremble. Her eyes rose to his face in bewilderment.

'You're really here?'

'Where else would I be?' Leaning forward, he kissed her with exquisite gentleness and then drew back.

'Cerys said she'd phoned and left a message for you, but I never expected you to come,' she said shakily, feeling the surge of heat that had started at her mouth and was rapidly gathering momentum as it flowed through her.

'I had to come. I needed to see for myself that you were all right.' He cupped her face, his fingers tracing the livid bruise on her temple, and Lowri felt her heart come to a halt when she saw the fear in his eyes. 'I was so afraid that you...you...'

He couldn't go on; the words were obviously too painful for him to utter. Lowri felt her heart give a massive leap before it began to race faster and faster. It couldn't be true—she must be dreaming. Vincenzo didn't love her. He couldn't do! And yet there was just something about the way he was looking at her...

Afterwards, she never knew where she had found the courage. Maybe if she had been thinking clearly, she wouldn't have done so but all of a sudden she found herself leaning towards him, pressing her mouth to his, *kissing* him with every scrap of the love she had stored away in her heart. There was a moment when he didn't move, a tiny fraction of time when his mouth went rigid under hers, and then the next instant he was kissing her back, kissing her as though his life depended on it too.

'I love you so much.' The words tumbled from his lips as he drew back and Lowri's heart soared. There wasn't a doubt in her mind that he was telling her the truth and it was so wonderful to hear it, to have her dreams come true.

'I love you too,' she told him, kissing his cheeks, his eyebrows, the tip of his elegant nose.

'You do? You really love me?' He stared at her and she laughed when she saw the shock in his eyes.

'Yes. Why? Don't you think I should love you?'

'No. I mean yes!' He pulled her into his arms and held her tight, so tight that she could feel his heart racing in time with hers. 'Hearing you say that you love me is what I have longed for but never thought would happen, so you must understand if I sound extremely shocked.'

'I never thought you would love me either,' she admitted. She drew back and looked into his eyes. 'I'm not sure if I'm dreaming this, Vincenzo, because it's what I wanted so much.'

'*This* isn't a dream, my darling.'

He kissed her hungrily, his mouth seeking a response she was only too eager to give. Lowri closed her eyes and let passion carry her to another dimension, a place where nothing mattered except her and Vincenzo.

And Megan and this baby she was carrying. A child she might miscarry.

Tears streamed down her cheeks and she felt him tense. He gently set her away from him, a frown darkening his brow when he saw her anguish. 'What is it, my darling? Tell me.'

'I'm pregnant but I may lose the baby because of the fall.'

Sobs choked her and she heard him sigh as he pulled her back into his arms. He rocked her to and fro, murmuring words she couldn't understand yet which comforted her all the same. He didn't try to stop her when she pulled away, simply offered her his handkerchief then sat beside her and took hold of her hand.

'Tell me what the doctor said, *tesoro*.'

Lowri told him word for word what the obstetrician had said. She didn't want to leave anything out, didn't want to raise his hopes and have to dash them if the worst happened. Vincenzo needed to know the truth, every bit of it.

'It was my own fault,' she said miserably. 'I wasn't concentrating and that's why I tripped. If I'd taken more care then it wouldn't have happened.'

'It's easy to be wise after the event,' he said softly. He turned her hand palm up and pressed his lips to the tender skin, making her shudder. 'Why were you so distracted?'

'Because I was thinking about what I was going to do.' She looked into his eyes. 'I was about to phone you and tell you my news.'

'And that worried you?' he queried, frowning.

'In a way, yes, it did.' She bit her lip.

'Because you were concerned about how I would react? But having another child was what we had hoped for.'

He sounded perplexed, as well he might. Lowri

took a deep breath, hoping she could make him understand. 'It was but I was scared about what it would mean.'

'That I would be a permanent part of your life and you weren't sure if that was what you wanted?' he suggested, his voice grating with pain.

'No!' She gripped his hand, needing to make him understand. 'I was afraid that it wasn't what *you* really wanted, that you would do it simply out of a sense of duty. I…I couldn't bear that, Vincenzo. The last thing I want is for me and the children to be a burden to you.'

'You could never be that.' He pulled her close and kissed her passionately. 'I need you so much, my darling. I can't bear to imagine my life without you and the children in it.'

'Really? You're quite sure?'

'I've never been more certain of anything in my life.' He kissed her again then pulled her to him, cradling her against him. 'I know that I told you I had never wanted children and it was true. I made up my mind that I wouldn't have a family very early on, mainly because my own childhood was less than idyllic.'

'Tell me about it,' she said softly, sensing that he needed to deal with the demons that had haunted him for far too long.

'I told you that my mother died when I was very young.' He carried on when she nodded and the lack of emotion in his voice told her how difficult he found it to talk about the past. 'My father made no secret of the fact that he bitterly resented having to look after me after she died. He was only interested in his work—in making more money—and the time he had to spend with me stopped him doing that.'

'How sad,' she said softly. 'You both missed out on so much.'

'Yes. I can see that now that I have Megan in my life as well as this new baby to look forward to.' He kissed her lightly then sighed. 'Anyway, I was sent away to school when I was seven and saw very little of him after that. Holidays were spent with my grandmother, who did her best to compensate for my father's lack of interest. However, it had a profound effect on me. I found it hard to get close to people and preferred my own company.'

'It was only natural after the way you were brought up,' she assured him.

'You think so?' He grimaced. 'Maybe you're right. However, I took it as a sign that I was exactly like my father. I couldn't bear the thought of inflicting the same unhappiness on my own children so I decided not to have any.'

'And you would have stuck to your decision if I hadn't turned up at your door and told you that you had a daughter.'

'Yes.' He smiled. 'I was so shocked it's a wonder I didn't pass out!'

'But you didn't, did you? You agreed to help me despite all your fears.' She lifted his hand to her face and held it against her cheek. 'Thank you so much, Vincenzo. I realise now just how much courage it took after hearing about your childhood.'

'I was surprised that I wanted to help,' he admitted. 'It sounds a terrible thing to say but I'd never really considered other people's needs before then. But when

I heard about Megan and how ill she'd been...well, I knew I wanted to help her.'

'Because inside you are a good person. You're nothing like your father—you wouldn't do the job you do if you were like him. You would be devoting your life to making money rather than saving lives.'

'Do you think so?' he said slowly.

'I know so.' She smiled at him. 'If you need proof, I would never have fallen in love with you if you were like him.'

He laughed as he pulled her to him. 'What can I say? I'm certainly not going to argue with you!'

He kissed her hungrily, only stopping when the door opened and Cerys and Megan appeared. Cerys looked from one to the other and grinned.

'No need to ask if you've sorted everything out. Good. Right. I am going to take Meg home with me for a sleep-over. I think you two could do with some time on your own.'

'Oh, but you don't have to do that,' Lowri began, but Cerys shook her head.

'Oh, but I do. Give Mummy and Daddy a kiss, sweetie, then we can go home and play Happy Families.' She grinned at them. 'It seems rather apt to me!'

Lowri blushed when Megan ran over to kiss her. She cuddled her close then let her go so she could kiss Vincenzo. Megan frowned as she stared at him.

'Are you really my daddy?'

'I am, *tesoro*. Is that all right with you?'

'Uh-huh. S'pose so.'

Megan ran back to Cerys, who laughed as she led her away. Vincenzo shook his head in amazement.

'That's it? She's quite happy to accept me as her daddy?'

'It appears so.' Lowri smiled at him. 'Children know instinctively who they can trust and Megan trusts you. As far as she's concerned you're her daddy and that's final. There's no going back on it now, Vincenzo.'

'And no way that I want to,' he growled, pulling her to him. 'I love you so much, my darling. I promise that I shall do everything in my power to make you and the children happy.'

'That's all anyone could ask,' she said, reaching up to kiss him.

She sighed blissfully when she felt his lips claim hers. No matter what happened, he would always be there for her and be there for Megan and any other children they had too. The future, which had seemed so scary just a few months ago, was suddenly filled with hope. Vincenzo loved her and together they would deal with whatever problems life threw at them.

EPILOGUE

Fifteen months later

LOWRI TUCKED A blanket around the baby sleeping in the pram. There was a breeze blowing up from the lake and she didn't want Giuliana Bethan to catch a chill. At six months old, she was growing rapidly and each day brought about new changes. Vincenzo's delight in his new daughter was a joy to see and Lowri never tired of watching them together. Despite his fears, Vincenzo was a natural when it came to looking after the children.

'Ah, so she's asleep, is she?'

He came out onto the terrace, putting his arms around her as he stared down at the newest addition to their family. Lowri smiled to herself when she saw the love on his face. He was as besotted with Giuliana as he was with Megan.

'Yes. She needs a nap so don't go picking her up or she'll be really cranky. Megan will want to play with her when she gets back from Maria's.'

He laughed. 'Megan really adores her, doesn't she?'

'She does. She was thrilled when I explained that

Giuliana had given her the special medicine that would help make her better.'

'We're so lucky,' Vincenzo said quietly. 'The fact that you didn't lose the baby was a miracle in itself and then to find out that she was a perfect match for Megan was wonderful. Having the stem-cell transplant means that Megan should live a long and healthy life.'

'Yes, we are. Very lucky indeed.' She turned into his arms, holding him close. 'We have to be the luckiest people in the world, Vincenzo. We have two beautiful children and we have each other. What more could we want?'

'Nothing,' he murmured as he covered her mouth with his. 'Absolutely nothing.'

* * * * *

Mills & Boon® *Hardback*
May 2014

ROMANCE

The Only Woman to Defy Him	Carol Marinelli
Secrets of a Ruthless Tycoon	Cathy Williams
Gambling with the Crown	Lynn Raye Harris
The Forbidden Touch of Sanguardo	Julia James
One Night to Risk it All	Maisey Yates
A Clash with Cannavaro	Elizabeth Power
The Truth About De Campo	Jennifer Hayward
Sheikh's Scandal	Lucy Monroe
Beach Bar Baby	Heidi Rice
Sex, Lies & Her Impossible Boss	Jennifer Rae
Lessons in Rule-Breaking	Christy McKellen
Twelve Hours of Temptation	Shoma Narayanan
Expecting the Prince's Baby	Rebecca Winters
The Millionaire's Homecoming	Cara Colter
The Heir of the Castle	Scarlet Wilson
Swept Away by the Tycoon	Barbara Wallace
Return of Dr Maguire	Judy Campbell
Heatherdale's Shy Nurse	Abigail Gordon

MEDICAL

200 Harley Street: The Proud Italian	Alison Roberts
200 Harley Street: American Surgeon in London	Lynne Marshall
A Mother's Secret	Scarlet Wilson
Saving His Little Miracle	Jennifer Taylor

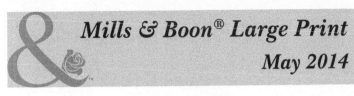

Mills & Boon® Large Print

May 2014

ROMANCE

The Dimitrakos Proposition	Lynne Graham
His Temporary Mistress	Cathy Williams
A Man Without Mercy	Miranda Lee
The Flaw in His Diamond	Susan Stephens
Forged in the Desert Heat	Maisey Yates
The Tycoon's Delicious Distraction	Maggie Cox
A Deal with Benefits	Susanna Carr
Mr (Not Quite) Perfect	Jessica Hart
English Girl in New York	Scarlet Wilson
The Greek's Tiny Miracle	Rebecca Winters
The Final Falcon Says I Do	Lucy Gordon

HISTORICAL

From Ruin to Riches	Louise Allen
Protected by the Major	Anne Herries
Secrets of a Gentleman Escort	Bronwyn Scott
Unveiling Lady Clare	Carol Townend
A Marriage of Notoriety	Diane Gaston

MEDICAL

Gold Coast Angels: Bundle of Trouble	Fiona Lowe
Gold Coast Angels: How to Resist Temptation	Amy Andrews
Her Firefighter Under the Mistletoe	Scarlet Wilson
Snowbound with Dr Delectable	Susan Carlisle
Her Real Family Christmas	Kate Hardy
Christmas Eve Delivery	Connie Cox

Mills & Boon® Hardback
June 2014

ROMANCE

Ravelli's Defiant Bride	Lynne Graham
When Da Silva Breaks the Rules	Abby Green
The Heartbreaker Prince	Kim Lawrence
The Man She Can't Forget	Maggie Cox
A Question of Honour	Kate Walker
What the Greek Can't Resist	Maya Blake
An Heir to Bind Them	Dani Collins
Playboy's Lesson	Melanie Milburne
Don't Tell the Wedding Planner	Aimee Carson
The Best Man for the Job	Lucy King
Falling for Her Rival	Jackie Braun
More than a Fling?	Joss Wood
Becoming the Prince's Wife	Rebecca Winters
Nine Months to Change His Life	Marion Lennox
Taming Her Italian Boss	Fiona Harper
Summer with the Millionaire	Jessica Gilmore
Back in Her Husband's Arms	Susanne Hampton
Wedding at Sunday Creek	Leah Martyn

MEDICAL

200 Harley Street: The Soldier Prince	Kate Hardy
200 Harley Street: The Enigmatic Surgeon	Annie Claydon
A Father for Her Baby	Sue MacKay
The Midwife's Son	Sue MacKay

Mills & Boon® Large Print
June 2014

ROMANCE

A Bargain with the Enemy	Carole Mortimer
A Secret Until Now	Kim Lawrence
Shamed in the Sands	Sharon Kendrick
Seduction Never Lies	Sara Craven
When Falcone's World Stops Turning	Abby Green
Securing the Greek's Legacy	Julia James
An Exquisite Challenge	Jennifer Hayward
Trouble on Her Doorstep	Nina Harrington
Heiress on the Run	Sophie Pembroke
The Summer They Never Forgot	Kandy Shepherd
Daring to Trust the Boss	Susan Meier

HISTORICAL

Portrait of a Scandal	Annie Burrows
Drawn to Lord Ravenscar	Anne Herries
Lady Beneath the Veil	Sarah Mallory
To Tempt a Viking	Michelle Willingham
Mistress Masquerade	Juliet Landon

MEDICAL

From Venice with Love	Alison Roberts
Christmas with Her Ex	Fiona McArthur
After the Christmas Party...	Janice Lynn
Her Mistletoe Wish	Lucy Clark
Date with a Surgeon Prince	Meredith Webber
Once Upon a Christmas Night...	Annie Claydon

Discover more romance at

www.millsandboon.co.uk

- ❤ WIN great prizes in our exclusive competitions
- ❤ BUY new titles before they hit the shops
- ❤ BROWSE new books and REVIEW your favourites
- ❤ SAVE on new books with the Mills & Boon® Bookclub™
- ❤ DISCOVER new authors

PLUS, to chat about your favourite reads, get the latest news and find special offers:

- 📘 Find us on facebook.com/millsandboon
- 🐦 Follow us on twitter.com/millsandboonuk
- ❤ Sign up to our newsletter at millsandboon.co.uk